REFLECTIONS
IN
DARK GLASS

The Life and Times of John Wesley Hardin

BRUCE McGINNIS

University of North Texas Press
Denton, Texas

Permissions
University of North Texas Press
P. O. Box 13856
Denton, Texas 76203

Library of Congress Cataloging-in-Publication Data

McGinnis, Bruce.
Reflections in dark glass : the life and times of John
Wesley Hardin / by Bruce McGinnis.
p.   cm.
ISBN 1-57441-008-3
1. Hardin, John Wesley, 1853–1895—Fiction. 2. Out-
laws—Texas—Fiction. I. Title.
PS3563.C364R44   1996
813' .54—dc20   95-26599
CIP

Cover design by Amy Layton
Cover photo of John Wesley Hardin from
the R. G. McCubbin Collection

This novel is a marriage of fiction and personal essay.
Although in many cases I have used actual settings, events,
people, and conversations (as recorded by participants
and later by historians), they are used fictitiously.
I have stood on the town square in Comanche and
tried to picture what went on that day in 1874
when John Wesley Hardin shot Charley Webb.
I have climbed the round-topped mesa that lies
several miles west of town and tried to imagine him
hiding out there and managing to avoid a
posse of a hundred or so men.
This book, then, is a product of my imagination.

Table of Contents

Preface

According to notes left by his son Will, in the late fall of 1900 when long-time Comanche County citizen Jim Stephens sat down to write of his friendship with "notorious" Texas bad man John Wesley Hardin, he had hoped to finish the project in short order, his general aim being to provide a brief factual record in narrative that would serve as a guide to Wes Hardin's life and thus counter the many misimpressions which unscrupulous authors and their sensational publications had spread abroad following Wes Hardin's death in 1895. A more immediate purpose was to provide a detailed, eyewitness account of the killing of Brown County Deputy Sheriff Charley Webb, an event that sorely troubled Mr. Stephens and which no author had yet represented to his satisfaction.

Some two years later, though he had managed to produce a fair though incomplete copy of his "record," Mr. Stephens despaired of accomplishing his original intentions. He lay this failure in part to his inability to defend his old friend against recent allegations that he had been not so much an outlaw as an unscrupulous and mean-spirited killer. This difficulty, in turn, prevented him from giving a comprehensive accounting either of Hardin or his actions. For example, though he was in command of the chronology of his associations with Hardin, he had been unable, he felt, to characterize accurately the complex relationships that made up Hardin's life, characterizations which he felt necessary to the construction of a richly textured whole that alone could do justice to Hardin and to their association. The principle relationships he had difficulty with were those Wes Hardin enjoyed with his father, J. G. Hardin, and with the family's Negro mammy, Julie Ola Faye, whose remembrances of the events of May 26, 1874, could have been impressions only on Mr. Stephens's part as he had no contact with Julie on that day and was never to see her again. Mr. Stephens especially despaired of dealing adequately with the events surrounding Charley Webb's death where Mr. Hardin was concerned, so private and enigmatic had the old man's responses been not just to his son's actions that fateful day but to the death of Webb as well. Only God, Mr. Stephens had told his son Will at the time, would have been able to write that side of the account with any accuracy. According to Will, a final difficulty Mr. Stephens wrestled with was his uncertain memory and the necessity of relying somewhat on John Wesley's accounting of the same events as set down in his autobiography.

Finally, in dejection, Mr. Stephens abandoned his reminiscence and destroyed what work he had completed—or so he led his family to believe. In going through his personal effects some months after his father's death in 1911, Will was surprised to discover an untitled manuscript, set down for the most part in his father's fine hand, of the proposed book on Wes Hardin. With only the early years of Wes Hardin's life accounted for and with parts of the text being scripted in a hand not his father's and the whole having no clear order or direction that he could discover, Will decided the manuscript was unfinished and of interest only to immediate family. For several years after its discovery, the material lay untouched in the bottom of a quilt box that sat at the foot of Will's bed. As he grew older, however, Will began to have second thoughts about the fate of his father's writings and set in once again to make sense of the manuscript and its confused contents, albeit with little success. Possessing no literary judgment or skill of his own, he passed the material on to an editor friend of his fathers, a Mr. George Bell, whose acquaintance his father had made on one of his excursions to New York to visit his sister. After looking over the materials, Mr. Bell advised Will to have the manuscript published privately, just as it had come into his hands, not based on any supposed literary value (indeed, as previously mentioned, though some parts of it were rather straightforward, others were jumbled almost beyond comprehension—the apparent confused recollections of Julie Ola Faye, for instance—and still others so wildly imaginative in their perspective and yet foreign to Mr. Stephens's temperament and style as a writer that, following Mr. Stephens's suggestion, perhaps only God could have written them) but rather to provide the firsthand account Mr. Stephens had wanted originally. Beyond that, Mr. Bell suggested, Will had no obligation other than allowing historians to make what use they could of the book after its publication. This plan Will determined to follow, as soon as funds were available. Unfortunately, Will died in 1939 with the manuscript still unpublished. From there it passed through a number of hands until it came into my possession following the death in 1990 of my grandmother Clara Ware, who was herself a lifelong resident of Comanche County and a Hardin before her marriage. After some study, I decided the manuscript worthy of wider distribution, if only for the reason given by Mr. George Bell when he first examined the work. In preparing the manuscript for publication, I placed the twenty-three odd sections in chronological sequence, as accurately as the evidence at hand would allow, and further took the liberty of giving a title to the whole as well as headings for the individual sections—here following, in this last, the implications arising from Mr. Stephens' comments to his son Will. Other than those additions, I have resisted the temptation to tinker with the remembrances of Mr. Stephens beyond correcting troublesome errors of grammar and spelling. The Julie Ola Faye sections, in particular, I have avoided changing (despite the difficulty these will pose for some readers) as they obviously represent Mr. Stephens's attempt to capture the authentic voice of his subject.

Bruce McGinnis
Amarillo, Texas

Jim Stephens

It was all a little strange the way it happened, the way I first learned about it. Even now, looking back, I sometimes cannot believe it did in exactly that way. We were leaving out of Chicago headed south, inching our way slowly through the outskirts of that impossibly large city, watching the stores and warehouses become fewer and wider apart the farther out we got. Finally, we saw only boarding houses and shacks, patched together with small garden plots in which occasionally stood two or three small children gawking in amused silence as the train, chugging out great puffy clouds of white steam, picked up speed and moved on into the open farm country ahead.

In the late summer of 1895, I was on my way back to Texas after spending over a month in Maine because of an illness in my sister's family. I had left my appointed seat and gone down to the smoker for a while before dinner, but not necessarily to smoke. Since leaving New York, I had found the smoker a quiet place to be alone and to rest. I could watch out the window without needing to think or, if I wanted, listen to the hypnotic rhythm of the iron wheels on the tracks as we rolled along.

Four, maybe five gentlemen were seated in the car when I came in, though I took no particular notice of their individual persons. They were talking quietly among themselves in the softly modulated voices so characteristic of men in that part of the nation, and I was interested only in finding a secluded spot where I could sit down and be alone for a few minutes before I ate. Taking a quick look at the available spaces, I picked an empty seat by a window some distance from the others. Here, I could watch the neatly arranged farms as they passed. I liked seeing their trim painted houses and outbuildings and the straightly plowed and planted fields, growing tall and green now under the hot August sun. Every mile or so, we passed a man or maybe a boy, and sometimes both, following a team of mules down the long straight rows of a mature corn field, pulling off the short fat ears of golden corn and tossing them into the bed of the wagon which the mules were pulling.

It was good to be going home. I felt I had been away too long, and although I had traveled extensively in the last few years and had each time enjoyed myself almost beyond measure, it was always nice to be headed back. The older a man gets, the more important it is to have a place to come back to. After he reaches a certain age, he may be reluctant to leave that place at all, no matter where he is going or what interest or excitement the journey may provide.

There was a time when I never thought I'd say that about the Comanche County of Texas, and certainly not about the town of Comanche itself. In fact, at one time I hated that little town and everyone in it. I can remember wanting to choke the life out of anyone who dared to say in my presence that Comanche might be a good place to live "if only the lowlife and niggers were cleared out of it." The locals were saying that a lot in the seventies and eighties and especially in the fall of '86 after the Negroes left.

But somewhere along the way I got over my anger, and I don't feel much of anything anymore. For some reason, even back then, I never left Comanche, and as the years rolled on I stopped thinking about what had happened to me and to my associates there so long ago. The terribly intense feelings that had been so important to me back then and that almost turned me into a lawless killer would have, had I given into them, undoubtedly brought about my death at a young age or else have put me in the state penitentiary at Huntsville for the remainder of my life. But time diminishes the importance of everything simply by wearing it away. Though I know I'm unlikely ever to forget the anger and hurt of those few hours and days when my life was so completely changed and brought down, looking back on it now I see all of it more clearly than I did then. I understand myself better also, and I realize a certain logic and inevitability lay in what happened. Sooner or later it was bound to happen, and a great deal of it may even have been my fault. I will never be able to forgive myself for that. Sometimes at night I can still see my friends hanging from the limb of that old Live Oak tree along with Joe Hardin. I can feel my uncle holding me back when I first heard what had happened so that I couldn't get my hands on a gun, and afterwards trying to quieten me down because he was afraid the mob was aiming to swing me, too. It was the same mob that earlier had murdered my brother in cold blood. Even now when I meet my brother's family on the streets of Comanche and look into the handsome faces of his grown sons, I am filled with remorse, although I'm sure Jake and Sam no longer blame me if in fact they ever did. They were too young then to remember their father, much less what happened to him and why.

Some say age and maturity and even pain are supposed to bring wisdom, and I suppose they do. In my case they can't have brought much. I sometimes find myself reliving the excitement and wonder of those rash times. The sense of glory and freedom which I felt strongly then, I am ashamed to confess, I am still attracted to from time to time, though eventually I did outgrow my tendency to give in to it. As I say, time heals many wounds, even great wounds. I look on Comanche as my home now, the place where I was born and where my roots are. Still, I have always wanted to put my impressions of Wes Hardin and what we knew together in writing, particularly the killing of Charley Webb, since his death marked the end of my association with Wes. It brought Wes to an end, also; and though I have considered often how others close to Wes responded to that fateful day—for example his father and Mama Julie Ola Faye, his second mother—I can speak only for myself. I would never presume, except in wildest imagination, to set down the complex emotions they must have felt when they first learned Wes had killed Charley Webb.

Jim Stephens

Sitting in the smoker beside the window, I was minding my own business and enjoying my pipe. I had my feet propped up on the opposite seat, and I was watching the small, square-cut farms go by sleek and pretty and all alike as peas in a pod, as Julie Ola Faye would have said. Perhaps that sameness or maybe the clackety-clack of the heavy iron wheels across the joints in the silver tracks had lulled me into something close to sleep. I may even have been asleep but with my eyes open and staring unseeing through the clean, shining glass. I'm not sure. What I do know is that for some time, I had been thinking about a girl I had loved when I was young and whose leaving had troubled me for years. At some point in my reverie I must have fallen asleep for a few seconds. When I opened my eyes again, I saw that one of the gentlemen I had noticed earlier had left his companions and moved into the seat across from mine. In a gesture of courtesy, I apparently had removed my feet from the seat, though I did not remember doing so. Upon further reflection, I realized that not only had he seated himself across from me, he had also asked me a question, which I was unable to recall.

"I'm sorry," I said in apology. "I must have been dozing. I've had rather a tiring trip. Would you mind repeating your question?"

"That's quite all right," the man replied, smiling. "I apologize myself. It was rather forward of me not to introduce myself first, but what I wanted to ask you was—"

But I'm getting ahead of myself. Let me explain about Wes first because if I don't make myself clear on that part then the rest of what I have to say won't make much sense.

Wes was born in Bonham, Texas, on May 26th, 1853. His father, J. G. Hardin, was a circuit-riding Methodist preacher and his mother, from all accounts, an attractive, intelligent, loving homemaker and wife. I can attest to that, as well as to the fact that she was an exceptional cook, especially of fried chicken and peach cobbler.

Wes had two brothers also, Joe and Jeff, and a sister, Mat. From the time of his birth until he was in his teens he led the kind of itinerant life required by his father's on-again, off-again profession, a life which included, in addition to the ministry, occasional school teaching and the practice of law. There were also frequent but temporary attempts at farming.

Despite these unlikely circumstances, Wes grew up a clever, rather perceptive boy as anyone who knew him well will testify, though he lacked the benefit of formal schooling as we know it today or even the company of educated friends. In addition, Wes also acquired in those first twelve or so years of his life the usual attitudes of a southern boy of his time and upbringing to the Negro question and Lincoln, to the war and Sherman, and to most figures of authority in general. Rather a normal upbringing for a boy of Wes's time and circumstances, I suspect, but here the course of Wes's life made an abrupt change.

In the fall of 1868 at the age of fifteen, Wes killed his first man. By the time he was twenty-one, six years later, he had killed some forty more, leaving their bodies bloodied and for the most part unburied along a line that ran from several points in Texas all the way to Kansas.

Forty men killed is a phenomenal number for one so young, or for one of any age for that matter, though I am persuaded that many may have killed that number or more in the war and with far less reason than Wes ever killed anyone. Some outlaws and highway men must have approached that number as well, if we only knew. At least in Wes's case it is also a number reflecting the violent, uncertain times in Texas in the twenty or so years after the war. Given those times and Wes's mercurial, charismatic temperament, could he have turned out other than he did? I often ask myself that question, and always I wind up admitting he could not have. The period of Reconstruction in Texas was one of the most unjust, repressive periods in the history of the nation, the problems of slavery and its moral consequences, notwithstanding. To illustrate that point, on April 22nd of 1873 when Governor Davis's hated state police were abolished by legislative vote, a member of the legislature John Henry Brown wrote in a letter to *The Dallas Herald* that "The people of the State of Texas are today delivered of as infernal an engine of oppression as ever crushed any people." Mr. Brown's voice was only one of many, a mighty chorus of anger and disillusionment, and Wes's voice was among them. Though it was a voice on occasion discordant, Wes had as much to do with bringing those dangerous, humiliating times to an end as any man in Texas.

Despite the good he may have accomplished, Wes was still a killer, as the several notches carved not into the grip of his old .44 but into a small willow stick he always carried on his person gave proof of. By the time of his imprisonment in October of 1878, he was reputed to have killed forty-four men, though if the truth were known, I believe the number who died under Wes's guns would be well beyond fifty. In making reference to his favorite pistol, I do not mean to imply that it was the only instrument used in all those killings. Other weapons were employed, of course, but I can bear witness that Wes was as talented with rifle or shotgun as with his pistol.

In 1873 Wes's family, including his two brothers and Joe's wife, moved to the county of Comanche in North Central Texas, leaving Wes to attend to his cattle business. In January of that next year, Wes arrived, having sent his young wife, Jane, on ahead to stay with his father and mother. On the morning of his twenty-first birthday, May 26th, after a successful day of horse racing and subsequent betting which won him over three thousand dollars in cash, Wes and some of his friends retired to John Wright's saloon on the northeast corner of the square in Comanche to try and spend as much of the money as possible on drink and gambling.

A few minutes later, with little forewarning either to himself or those with him, he was accosted outside the saloon by Brown County Deputy Sheriff Charley Webb, a fool-hearted individual evidently looking to build up his reputation by being the man either to kill the notorious John Wesley Hardin or to bring him into jail. After being drawn upon first and shot in the side, Wes subsequently took out his own pistol and shot and killed Webb. As soon as he could after he surrendered his gun to Comanche County Sheriff John Carnes, he took his knife from his pocket and carved one more notch into that smooth, round willow stick.

Though the shooting seemed to me and to others who witnessed it an obvious one of self-defense, the death of Charley Webb was to bring Wes's family and friends more sorrow than the other forty or so killings together. It would also lead some four years later to his arrest, trial, and eventual imprisonment. That outcome was classic irony, as the circumstances of the shooting were as well documented as any Wes was involved in; but I should also add that to the best of my knowledge Wes never wantonly killed anyone except in self-defense, though I will admit that he extended that word *defense* to include not only his life but also a rather narrow sense of personal dignity. Yet, despite his reputation for rash action, Wes had literally hundreds of friends including several men in the profession of law as well as other people high in position and respect. He also never held up a bank or robbed a train or otherwise stole for money. He didn't have to. He was remarkably skilled at both gambling and horse racing and usually carried on his person large sums of money gained in those endeavors. In addition, he was not averse to earning an honest dollar for an honest day's labor. But don't mistake my intention. I am not trying to make Wes out as any kind of hero. Although he was as good a friend as I have ever had, he was also a hot-blooded killer with little or no compunction or regret.

Although Wes escaped that day in Comanche, the end was in sight. Shortly after the Webb shooting, he became the object of the largest manhunt—totaling at one point a loose posse of over five hundred men—ever to be organized in Texas. For the next three years, the threat of his return caused so much fear and terror in Comanche itself that the town resembled an armed camp in much the same way the entire county had some fifteen years before when the threat of warring and raiding Comanche Indians was at its height.

Wes was finally trailed to Florida by Texas Rangers, then to Alabama, where he was arrested and brought back to Texas to stand trial. On September 28, 1878, in the town of Comanche, he was sentenced to twenty-five years at hard labor in the penitentiary at Huntsville for the killing of Charley Webb, though numerous witnesses testified that Webb had not only fired first but had provoked the encounter to begin with. Although this particular killing was Wes's most sensational and focused the public's attention on him not only in Texas but all over the nation to the extent that it led to his eventual capture, this is not to say that those first six years and ensuing forty other killings were without their appropriate terror and drama. I should know. I was his friend and present at a good many of them. And who can tell? Maybe in the turmoil and confusion of battle, especially at night, by rights a few of those notches cut into that willow tally stick should have been mine. I certainly did my share of the shooting, but don't get me wrong. I make no claim to any of them. I want only to get my view of the story as straight as I can.

Jim Stephens

Let me start over. At least let me start from the beginning and fill in the gaps. That way I will feel I have done a good job, and maybe there won't be many questions at the end.

I don't know. In the past I never wanted to talk about Wes. In fact, I refused whenever I was asked. As I've grown older, however, I've become largely disassociated from the experiences we had together, and I see them for the curiosities they were. I now enjoy discussing them occasionally and hearing others express their minds about them, though I keep myself out of the account as much as I can. Increasingly, I find such reflection to have therapeutic value rather in the manner of a confession. But that is another issue.

Several years ago, in late August of 1895, I had been to Maine to visit my sister, whose husband died during my stay, following a lingering and painful illness. Having stopped briefly in Chicago to renew an old acquaintance, I was returning to Texas on the train. At the time I was seated in a smoking car with a number of other gentlemen, and we were somewhat west of Chicago, heading south toward St. Louis where I planned to make a third visit, although a short one of only a day or so.

Perhaps noticing my reluctance to enter into the general conversation, one of the gentlemen seated himself in front of me and as a gesture of courtesy inquired concerning the nature of my trip.

"I'm going home," I responded, after he had repeated his question.

"Oh, is that so?"

"Yes, I have been up to New England to visit my sister and am now on my way back to Texas. I also spent a few days in Chicago with—"

"Oh, really! Texas?"

At the mention of my destination, the gentleman's expression underwent a most extraordinary change. I can't describe it, but the coloring of his skin actually deepened. A flush of excitement spread over his pale face, and his eyes, which I remember as being rather dull and common, began to burn with a sharp intensity.

"Yes."

"How interesting! How utterly fascinating!"

Everyone in the car now turned to look at me, their eyes wide and singularly inquisitive. Small sighs of amazement escaped their lips and animated their faces. It was as if I had admitted to being a freak or had identified myself as the man who killed President Lincoln, though I would have been only ten years old at the time. This curious behavior on the part of my inquisitor and his associates was not entirely a surprise to me, however, as I had observed something of the same attitude in New York and to a lesser degree almost everywhere my travels had taken me. At the close of the century, anyone known to be from the far west or to have intimate knowledge of that part of the nation was still somewhat of a sensation in the East among many people. It was a response I had grown used to, and I thought I was seeing it yet again, though a few minutes later I found out how wrong that assumption was.

By now the gentleman across from me had recovered himself enough to continue.

"What part of Texas?" he asked. "What city?"

A faint smile started on the right side of his mouth and moved slowly across to the left. For a moment I thought he might be leading me on.

"Oh, not a city at all," I said, "only a small town, hardly

big enough to have a name. You wouldn't know it."

"I might," he said politely. "What town?"

"Comanche. It's a little place in Central Texas, actually a county with a town of the same name as county seat."

"Comanche, indeed!" he exclaimed. "Well! Well! What do you know! Well, bless my soul. Now this is a coincidence."

Once again, I was taken aback by the intensity of his response to what I had just said. What is more, some of the other men were expressing similar sentiments, though in muted tones. By that I knew I had been wrong to attribute their earlier interest entirely to romantic notions about the west. I detected too much of surprise in their demeanor but also what I took to be hostility and perhaps anger.

Looking back, I can see I had not moved as far from the past as I thought. How difficult it is to lose one's old fearful mistrust about people and their motives, especially when those impressions were formed when one was young and in juxtaposition to uncertain and rather dangerous circumstances. Perhaps being attendant upon my brother-in-law's decline and death, plus seeing my sister's suffering, affected me more than I knew and I was simply overreacting, but for a group of strangers on a train to act as these had done to the mention of a small town in Texas—well, it made me wish I had my pistol tucked in my belt. I would have felt safer and more relaxed, as well.

"It's only a small town," I protested. "It's not—"

"Yes, I understand," my companion said, sensing my uneasiness. "It's simply that we'd been talking about Comanche before you came in."

"You had?"

"Yes, we had. We were just remarking what an interesting place it must have been back in the sixties and seventies. Is it still that way?"

"What way? You mean interesting?"

"Well, the violence mostly—all that violence we've heard about."

The gentleman went on to ask me polite questions

concerning the history of the county, especially its reputation for Indian trouble after the war, as well as its notoriety in dealing with the Negro problem in the eighties. I decided he must have read an article about Texas which contained random comments about Comanche County. I couldn't think of another explanation. In order not to appear uncooperative, I responded as straightforwardly as I could without, however, volunteering information beyond what I was asked.

"By the way, that's the town where they finally brought the notorious John Wesley Hardin to trial, isn't it?"

I don't remember what I expected the man to ask me next, but I would never have guessed it to be a question about Wes. My own surprise at this point must have been as evident to the gentleman as it was paralyzing to me. Not only could I not answer immediately, I could not think.

"Yes, I suppose it was," I said at last, feigning a disinterest I obviously didn't feel.

By now a couple of other men had left their seats and taken up positions allowing them access to the conversation. Meanwhile, I had composed myself enough to continue my guise of casualness to good effect, or so I believed. First one gentleman and then another went on to speculate about what to them must have seemed the greatest wonder west of the Mississippi—the largest concentration of sheer lawlessness and violence since the war, and that located in one individual, John Wesley Hardin. I had no choice but to sit until they had finished, looking politely interested and not too puzzled, while in fact I was amazed how exaggerated the facts of Wes's life had become. Much of the information they related had obviously been conjecture on the part of the writer of the article I assumed they had read.

"I also heard he was reformed," one of the men pointed out. "I heard that in prison he studied law and educated himself."

"That's what they say," I agreed, wanting to corroborate that one correct fact.

"Then it's really too bad about El Paso," the man said.

"Even after the life he led and the people he killed, it is still too bad."

Jim Stephens

"What about El Paso?" I asked, struggling to remain calm. "What's too bad? What about John Wesley?"

The gentleman's remark could hardly have hit me harder. Something was wrong. Something was bad wrong. I knew I was acting too concerned for a man who only minutes before had been a seemingly disinterested listener and a reluctant one at that, but the whole experience had unnerved me. I was not at my best.

"Here, Sir," one of the men said, taking a Chicago morning paper off the seat beside him and thrusting it out to me. "Here, read it for yourself."

At first, I didn't want to take the paper, nor did I want to know what it said. I figured I already knew, and I was afraid of what I would find. But I could hardly refuse it, and then I saw it, just as I had expected, and bigger than life too. In large bold type the headlines screamed out their sensational news—notorious outlaw and killer John Wesley Hardin was dead, a victim of the same gun-violence which had been his life. Below the headline was a photo of a man purported to be John Wesley Hardin. He was stretched out on a table with his shirt off and with the bullet holes showing like weeping, angry eyes in his head and body. But I didn't immediately recognize the man in the picture. It had been too long. My first thought was *No, this is a mistake! That's not Wes Hardin in the picture. That's someone calling himself Wes Hardin, someone who subsequently got himself shot for his lying and boasting.*

But as I examined the photo more closely, remembering what I knew, I had to conclude that it might indeed be Wes. It had been more than twenty years since I had seen him. He had been twenty-one then, a young, handsome man in his prime. He would now be well over forty, an age which the man in the picture definitely had reached. It just might be Wes. In fact, it probably was. As much as I wanted to deny it, I knew in my heart that Wes was dead.

Underneath the photo was an El Paso *Daily Herald* article dated August 20th, 1895, containing the following account:

> Last night between 11 and 12 o'clock, San Antonio street was thrown into an intense state of excitement by the sound of four pistol shots that occurred at the Acme saloon. Soon the crowd surged against the door, and there, right inside, lay the body of John Wesley Hardin, his blood flowing over the floor and his brains oozing out of a pistol shot wound that had passed through his head. Soon the fact became known that John Selman, constable of Precinct No. 1, had fired the fatal shots that had ended the career of so noted a character as Wes Hardin, by which name he is better known to all old Texans. For several weeks past trouble has been brewing and it has been often heard on the streets that John Wesley Hardin would be the cause of some killings before he left the town.
>
> Only a short time ago Policeman Selman arrested Mrs. McRose, the mistress of Hardin, and she was tried and convicted of carrying a pistol. This angered Hardin and when he was drinking he often made remarks that showed he was bitter in his feelings towards Selman. Selman paid no attention to these remarks, but attended to his duties and said nothing. Lately, Hardin had become louder in his abuse and had continually been under the influence of liquor and at such times

he was very quarrelsome, even getting along badly with some of his friends. This quarrelsome disposition on his part resulted in his death last night and it is a sad warning to all such parties that the rights of others must be respected and that the day is past when a person having the name of being a bad man can run rough shod over the law and rights of other citizens. This morning a *Herald* reporter started after the facts and found John Selman, the man who fired the fatal shots, and his statement was as follows:

"I met Wes Hardin about 7 o'clock last evening close to the Acme Saloon. When we met Hardin said, 'You've got a son that is a bastardly, cowardly s—of a B——.'

"I said: 'Which one?'

"Hardin said: 'John, the one that is on the police force. He pulled my woman when I was absent and robbed her of $50, which they would not have done if I had been there.'

"I said: 'Hardin, there is no man on earth that can talk about my children like that without fighting, you cowardly s—of a B——.'

"Hardin said: 'I am unarmed.'

"I said: 'Go get your gun. I am armed.'

"Then he said, 'I'll go and get a gun and when I meet you I'll meet you smoking and make you pull like a wolf around the block.'

"Hardin then went into the saloon and began shaking dice with Henry Brown. I met my son John and Capt. Carr and told them I expected trouble when Hardin came out of the saloon. I told my son all that had occurred, but told him not to have anything to do with it, but to keep on his beat. I also notified Capt. Carr that I expected trouble with Hardin. I then sat down on a beer keg in front of the Acme saloon and waited for Hardin to come out. I insisted on the police force keeping out of the trouble because it was a personal matter between Hardin and myself. Hardin had insulted me personally.

"About 11 o'clock Mr. E.L. Shackleford came along and met me on the sidewalk. He said: 'Hello, what are you doing here?'"

"Then Shackleford insisted on my going inside and taking a drink, but I said, 'No, I do not want to go in there as Hardin is in there and I am afraid we will have trouble.'

"Shackleford then said: 'Come on and take a drink anyway, but don't get drunk.' Shackleford led me into the saloon by the arm. Hardin and Brown were shaking dice at the end of the bar next to the door. While we were drinking I noticed that Hardin watched me very closely as we went in. When he thought my eye was off him he made a break for this gun in his hip pocket and I immediately pulled my gun and began shooting. I shot him in the head first as I had been informed that he wore a steel breast plate. As I was about to shoot the second time some one ran against me and I think I missed him, but the other two shots were at his body and I think I hit him both times. My son then ran in and caught me by the arm and said: 'He is dead. Don't shoot any more.'"

Below that was another account signed by F. F. Patterson, the bartender of the Acme Saloon:

"My name is Frank Patterson. I am a bartender at—. Hardin was standing with his back to Mr. Selman. I did not see him face around before he fell or make any motion. All I saw was that Mr. Selman came in the door, said something and shot and Hardin fell—. The first shot was in the head."

And below that another:

"My name is H. S. Brown. I am in the grocery business. . . . When the shot was fired Mr. Hardin was against the bar, facing it, as near as I can say, and his back was towards the direction the shot came from. I did not see him make any effort to get his six-shooter."

And finally:

"The wounds on Hardin's body were on the back of the head, coming out just over the left eye. Another shot in the right breast, just missing the nipple, and another through the right arm. The body was embalmed by Undertaker Powell and will be interred at Concordia at 4 P.M."

I don't know what I felt when I finished reading the paper. It was shock, to be sure, but I don't believe it was remorse. If it was, it wasn't for Wes himself, but for the fact he had not had a chance to defend himself. I hadn't seen him since 1874, and when he was arrested and brought back to Comanche, I didn't attend his trial. At the time I feared for my personal safety and thought it expedient not to tempt the mob who had murdered my brother, at least six members of which I expected to be sitting on the jury. It wasn't sadness I felt either. I had long ago put Wes out of my mind. Our association had existed for an immediate purpose. When that was ended and Wes was sent to prison, that part of my life was over. For the briefest of moments after reading the articles, I regretted the loss of the excitement and danger of those early times, but it was not possible to recapture them, nor did I wish to. A new century was about to be born, and men like Wes and the deeds they perpetrated belonged to another time, an old and dying time. This was a new time with different needs and different dreams. I was a part of it, and Wes was not. He was of the past and the past was gone. John Selman's back-shooting gun had slammed the door on it.

Anonymous

The man came slowly up the long rows moving south by slightly southwest, approaching almost imperceptibly a line of squat broad oaks that sat grafted into the large sand dump thrown up by the wind along the edge of the field. Looking at a distance like giant toadstools, the great oaks ran east and west for half a mile, being the south boundary of the field. The east, west, and north boundaries, running a similar half mile and forming a near perfect square, contained the same giant green toadstools as if the field were a cow chip rotted into dust but still supporting at its perimeters a rich, parasitic growth.

The trees were the solemn, haunting reminder of a once sizeable woods which only twenty-five years before had been savagely hacked and burned and the resulting field grubbed clean by the original owner, whose hopes and dreams for the field had ended abruptly somewhere in Virginia by a musket ball to the head in the summer of '63.

The present occupant had been on the place less than a year and was now intently involved in some laborious activity that to an unknowing observer seemed to require considerable starting and stopping, not to mention periodic turning from side to side and occasional stooping as if a large bug were trying to execute a two legged crawl using alternate legs until its movements sideways and vertical equaled and even surpassed those forward. Observers more knowledgeable, however, would not have had to look at all to say what the man was doing or why he was doing it. In fact, given the time of year, they would have been surprised to hear he was doing anything else. Most likely they were doing it themselves or soon would be. Cotton, or rather the promise of it, explained everything.

At one time the whole field had been under plow, and on any given day in the spring of the year as many as a dozen hands, mostly Negro, could have been seen dotting its landscape like so many toiling though reluctant ants engaged in the same starting and stopping and turning and stooping. Now only a portion of the field, perhaps fifty acres, was in active cultivation, though the absence of the laborers was more physical than actual. Their presence seemed somehow still to prevail, pervading the quietness of the field and its confines, hanging bodiless though silent above the muted beds. The war, of course, had changed everything, and now only the man's solitary figure remained, with a second figure down near the beginning of the rows on the north end still too uncertain in either shape or size to be much more than a lump patched onto the brilliant white of the field.

Earlier the man had been only a dark stick himself, bound into vague inactivity, distant and indistinct upon the flat, pale immensity of the field. Because of the dark color of his clothes, he had appeared no more than a pencil mark on a large square of white paper, despite the methodic rise and fall of the hoe. As he came on, his hesitant yet anxious steps vanished beneath him, swallowed by the soft obscurity of the waning afternoon out of which he had first emerged. Gradually, his stature increased in bulk and height; and he gained, as he neared the upper end of the long rows of newly planted cotton, the embodied figure of a full-sized man. He was dressed in a faded black suit worn thin with use and repeated washing. Despite his labor, the suit appeared clean and pressed and was apparently free of any sweat or its stain. He walked easily, almost gracefully, but with a slight limp, a result not of physical disability but of too many years behind a mule-propelled plow with one foot down into the furrow and the other upon the resulting bed so that now he walked that way even on level ground.

The man was thin but hard muscled, and the suit hung on him as it might upon an iron post, with the shape and obduracy of the iron showing beneath the cloth. His hands below the sleeves on his coat were large and knotted, while his face above the mouth was cold and stiff, like flint, though his eyes were the soft blue of a summer afternoon. In sympathy, the expression around his mouth was kind and compassionate, supporting a gentle, disarming smile as of something amusing but slightly ironic. He was well tanned and unbearded, tall and straight, a man of approximately middle age, though the hair which fell from under his hat and lay curled upon his shoulders lacked any trace of discoloration or aging. An exquisite honey yellow, it shone like gold in the afternoon sun.

Behind him the second figure came on, chopping and thinning in the young cotton the same as the man, pulling the large clumps of goose grass out into the center of the rows where later under the midday sun it would wrinkle, curl in on itself, and die.

The second figure was a woman of maybe forty years and certainly not less than two hundred pounds. If anything, she worked in more obvious, hesitant and labored complaint than the man. She was a big woman with bare, brawny arms and a generous chest upon which hung like twin sacks of feed two remarkable breasts, though she was not given to fat, only to sheer size until she seemed to have God's plenty in double proportions. Downward across her simple, pretty face, dark sweat rolled in thick sweet rivers to fall unhindered into the open cleavage of her great bosom. There it collected in pools so that the front of her thin flowered dress from her waist upward was stained with fine brown dust, and the protruding nipples of her breasts showed plainly through the cloth, two rich chocolate moons pasted onto an expanse as dark and vast as the sky at night. She had correspondingly plump, thrusting buttocks and thick plunging thighs and, in abundance, a soft loamy womanness that bound her to the rich fertile ground upon which she toiled with wide bare feet.

And she was black, almost indescribably black, so much so that the softer gray of her eyes seemed to gleam out of the mouths of caves. Despite her state, she appeared a proud woman and, like her companion, kind and compassionate.

By now the man had reached the end of the row and turned back to the woman. He was engaged in clearing off her rows along the ends, cleaning them for maybe ten steps along so that when she reached that point she could simply turn and start down two more. On his head he wore a broad brimmed, faded black hat that shadowed his face. From time to time he took the hat off and, using a large handkerchief he kept in the inside breast pocket of his coat, wiped the sweat from his brow. So like the suit was the hat in wear and fadedness that it might have been fashioned from the same cloth and undergone an equal number of wearings and subsequent washings.

The man cut a striking figure, and for a moment in silhouette he might have been Moses in the deserts of Sinai and the woman he stood watching one of the chosen of Jehovah. It was a comparison the man had noted himself, but one he did not enjoy making, for like Moses he watched not just his people but also the far horizons of the past for the known enemy behind, and the vast ones of the future for the unknown in front. It was the insight of a moment, but in that moment the old troubled watchfulness came also into his face and eyes. He was a man who had journeyed and now was tired. He had come at the end of many days to this small spot of ground where he hoped to establish himself and his people with him.

Always a gentle loving man, he had nevertheless been hardened over the years by violence and retribution until he was truly a man of his time and place—the frontier of Texas in 1874. Though he was still filled with the soft gentle love of his young manhood, he had been steeled by years of wandering through deserts of danger and uncertainty, looking for a sign in the heavens to lead him and his people to a land of peace and plenty. Now, looking out toward the woman and beyond, he thought, *I have come a far way. Though this land is not the land I would have chosen, it is the land where for the moment I am. For the sake of my family who may one day know a better land, I have accepted it for what it is. Maybe here in all the earth, I will be able to stop. Maybe here I can set myself down and just live without looking always over my shoulder for whoever may be wanting to harm me or one of my family, whether it is Reconstruction Niggers, State Police or Texas Rangers. Maybe this is the spot the Lord has picked. Here in this place I will rest and serve Him and here in His good time I will die and be interred. Blessed be the name of the Lord. Amen! Yes, a far way, a long journey, and now I am tired.*

The thoughts were in the man's head and for the briefest of moments there on his face. Then they were gone, leaving him blank, waiting and patient. Yet, above him in the late afternoon air, awash with the warming sun, an aura of thundering violence still flashed and sounded—haggard figures, pale and slight, galloping on specter mounts, swords and rifles uplifted, screaming in furious terrible silence their blood curdling cries; men slamming to a halt, their horses' heads thrown back, caught up, teeth bared and foaming, and there dismounting quickly to throw a rope over the nearest stout limb and as quickly to put a man's neck in it and jerk it up and tie it off and as quickly to mount again and ride like death into the dusky twilight, cackling their wild savage laughter, off in search of other limbs and other necks. And through it all, the man just waiting. Accepting. Patient.

Suddenly from behind the woman and to her side, though she was still at some distance, a third, shorter figure appeared and then a fourth. It was as if, hidden by her bulk and pace, they had grown out of the very dust through which she walked, to materialize from nothing into something like in the old myth—now let there be two more. One was a child, a boy of not more than seven or eight, a Negro like her; the other, a great white dog of considerable size, though as much of width and length as of height. Together they moved across one middle and began to walk parallel with the woman, toward where the man was standing at the end of the rows watching them come.

It was a scene from any of the last one hundred years in the South and from almost any of its states, though it was now some ten years since the ending of the war and more than that since cotton had been in its glory time. Since the war, however, the scene had shifted. It now lay west across the Mississippi, near the geographical center of Texas. It had changed too, as well as moved. The man in the black suit now chopped in the cotton alongside the woman rather than merely watching only as he would have done in the past.

But it was still cotton, the new dream as it had been the old, and the land was new and fresh, not old and wasted. This was Texas, not Mississippi or Alabama, and it was 1874, not '44 or even '64. Men had found new ways to spend their time and get paid for it. Cattle was one of them. Random violence was another.

The man no longer watched the woman and her escorts now as he had done for the last several moments, leaning on his hoe while he waited. He had shifted his attention to another matter. His head and eyes were now turned east where above the row of oaks on that side of the field a tall column of soft brown smoke could be seen rising into the cloudless sky. It was a thousand feet in the air by the time he first noticed it, and vertical like a chimney. Now it had begun to drift ever so slightly northeast.

The man lifted his hand to his eyes, though they were shaded already by the hat, and squinted intently as he tried to read in the smoke some indication where and what and possibly even who and why. After a minute, he thought, *That would be just about the center of town, just about right on the square, except it ain't no courthouse. It ain't even a very large building 'cause the smoke aint that black nor yet is it fierce enough, though some kind of building or similar structure it definitely is. Or maybe it's that old oak on the southwest corner*

*where Martin Fleming hid out from the Indians when he was
young. But at least it ain't that. It ain't Comanches for sure.
Not even Comanches would try to burn down a whole town
and on race day at that. If it were even possible it was
Comanches, I would not now be hoeing in this field minus one
gun around my waist and another one slung over my shoulder
on a strap. No, it has got to be a building of some kind.*

By this time the smoke was beginning to blacken a little,
again signing to the man more of where and what, though not
yet clearly of who and why. *Yes,* he thought, *it is almost on the
square in Comanche. Maybe it is even a wagon or two of them
and maybe they have feed in them, and that's what it is. But it
is sure enough beginning to look like some building, though I
swear if I can think which one it is. Or worse. But what worse
I will not consider now. Whatever it is, John Carnes can handle
it, or if he can't alone there are plenty of good men close by who
can, including my son Joe.*

The man turned back now, his hand falling away from his
face to flap softly down against the side of his thigh like the
bony wing of a large bird, again watching the woman and her
steadily advancing progress along with that of the boy and
the great dog. The dog was in front now, plodding slowly along
on large broad paws in a peculiar rhythmic, rolling gait
through the deep level sand, more like a bear than a dog.

After a moment, the man turned again and walked out to
the edge of the field where a wagon sat hitched to two mules,
one pure white like the dog and the other dark brown to almost
black, and both asleep. Upon gaining the front of the wagon,
the man reached up under the seat stanchion and hauled out
a large crock jar wrapped in a damp, dirty brown tow sack
and tied off around the middle and top with a straw colored
piece of binding twine. He removed the cork and, lifting the
jar, drank long and deep. He drank for half a minute,
swallowing steadily without taking a breath, his Adam's apple
moving up and down on the otherwise stilled surface of his
throat until finally he broke free of the sucking jug to take in
great quick breaths of air. Lowering the jug, he replaced the

cork and sat it back under the seat. He stood a moment longer until he could gain his breath, and then he turned again to look back at the smoke, gave it a furtive glance and then dismissed it, thinking, *It could not possibly concern me. Maybe some folks have time to set fires and then to watch them burn, but other folks have to work. Maybe I should go ahead and add, "Even lucky enough to have to work." But whatever it is it doesn't concern me, and I refuse to be bothered with it, so it is a standoff. It is too far and the wind is from the wrong direction for it to burn over this way, and by the time I woke up one of them mules and got him out of the harness and into town, most likely it wouldn't be a fire any longer. Besides, I have got to quit soon anyway and go into town because I told Wesley I would come in on his birthday and buy him a drink and afterwards we could have supper with Jane and all the family. I can see where it was when I get to town, but right now I have got to stay in this field.*

Now, the man turned and mounted the wagon. After he had settled into the seat, he reached into his middle and from somewhere beneath the faded coat withdrew a wrinkled leather-covered Bible and began to read, turning slowly almost tenderly the soft fine sheets, running his finger along the lines while he read down the page. He read for some time, leaning back against the seat and not looking at the woman, not even when she reached the end of her rows.

Instead of turning and starting back down, the woman stopped and spoke the single phrase, "Masta Johnny." It was not his name. It was not even what he liked to be called. It was simply the name she had used for over fifteen years now, and she refused to relinquish it.

The woman said the man's name only once, and softly, but it was as if the man could hear again the thin thundering figures come charging from the black past, demanding and grotesque, their nooses swinging widely, their dark steeds foaming blood and fear. But it was not the softness in her voice that brought him back to himself, but the piggy-backed sound of "Masta Johnny" tinged with urgency. He looked up then with such quickness and directness that his head seemed to snap on his neck, and when it did come up it was not toward the woman but east toward the woods and the smoke. It was as if her voice had said also, *Look there, Masta, to the east where the turn row becomes a rutted sand trail and vanishes into the dark of the trees. Look quick, 'cause somethin' is wrong. Somethin' is sho bad wrong.*

And the man did look, but at first he could see nothing he should not have seen. Then after a moment, he saw the hunched figure racing along the dark overgrown lane about to emerge from the surrounding gloom into the bright light of the late afternoon sun. He stared intently now at the gap in the wooded row which signaled the emergence of the lane from the woods, his brown face wrinkled in concern, thinking, *So you were wrong. That fire didn't need wind or even time, not when it could find someone to gather it up in a basket and bring it four miles on a horse to where I am trying to work and occasionally read my Bible.*

Then the full figure of the horse and its rider burst out of the line of trees, moving without jolt or sound as if still only a thought in the man's mind, a nameless horror in the shape of a horse and its rider, though still curiously dreamlike and disembodied, coming on silently through the soft deep sand with incredible speed and purpose. Without looking at the woman, the man said aloud, "Yes, you are right. Something is wrong. Something is sure enough bad wrong."

Jim Stephens

Although Wes and I had known each other for several years, our relationship did not become close until the spring of '67. Wes was fourteen; I was twelve, and he was my hero because he knew so much more than I did and was generous in sharing what he knew. He could also handle both a six-shooter and a rifle better than any other man I had ever known or would ever know, for that matter. I don't know where he learned that skill, although I suspect he taught himself. Neither his father nor his brothers were ever that interested.

But it was the guns themselves Wes was attracted to rather than the fact that they shot lead bullets and could be used to kill other men. He was drawn to their history and the tradition that stood behind them and was fascinated by the way they worked and the particular kind of genius that had gone into the design of their mechanisms. It was almost as if, just by handling a gun, he was paying allegiance to that genius. It was an obligation in trust to be capable of using one as well as it was possible to use it. Wes had first mentioned the dedication he felt in this respect while we were still in school, but back then I wasn't old enough to understand what he meant.

"Jimmy, son," Wes would say, "a gun is no more than a steel glove that you slip on your hand just as you would a leather one. When you come to look on using a gun in that way, you find that it is not something you have to think about.

It is always there just as your hand is always there. It moves and shoots itself naturally, and from any position. It does so without mistake or miscalculation. It's just like you have never had to explain to your hand how to take hold of an object or to say to that hand, 'Pick up that chalk and hold it just so and write words with it' or 'Lay down that particular card in just that certain way.' You don't have to do it because the hand already knows. You never had to teach it. You never even had to think about it. Whatever your hand can do, a steel glove fitted to that hand will not hinder."

I'll bet I heard Wes say that or something similar to it a hundred times. In addition to the talk, he was always wanting to teach me to handle a pistol the way he did, but I could never get it down. I lacked his quickness and agility. Despite spending hours and hours practicing, I could never do it. Handling a gun the way Wes did it is a gift from God. It's a calling just like the ministry is a calling. I just never heard the call. Years later when some were saying what a blood-thirsty killer Wes was, with no compassion or breeding, I would think how he had been an artist and the gun no more than the bright brush he held in his hand and the killings just brush strokes onto a composition in red. Back then I told myself that one day he would be understood and appreciated for the master he was. And back then I believed it. Wes never looked on a gun as something to kill with or even as a way of making himself more of a man. To him it was just a way of expressing himself. It was like clarity of enunciation or a gesture such as you might make with your hand. It was a gift, a calling. He tried to teach it to me, but I could never learn it.

It wasn't just guns. I used to follow Wes everywhere he went and make every move he made. There was nothing we didn't try, and I guess he taught me just about everything I know that was ever of any use to me. I don't mean just about horses and guns and gambling and women but about honesty and truth and discipline, too. It was a good time to be growing up, and Wes was the best friend I could have had. I have never regretted those early years. Even now when I look back on them, it's as though they were yesterday. It's as though we had just come in from a long night of following the dogs along the black darkness of the creek and we would be scratched up and bleeding a little and tired and happy all at the same time. Then we would go inside and get in our beds to sleep, and I would lie for a long time staring up into the quiet dark, listening to the dogs trying to settle down outside in the yard. I would be thinking how tired I was and how happy and how much fun it had all been. Then in the morning when I wake up, it is thirty years later and I am a man and no longer a boy. All that with Wes was another time and place.

When my mother first got sick in '63, Pa sent my sister Jill and me to Trinity County to live with my uncle and his wife and their three children, who were near our ages. Although this was my sister's first extended visit to Sumpter, I had spent a part of every summer there since '61, visiting my cousins. It was in that year I first met John Wesley and spent some time with him. When my mother recovered somewhat, we came home. I don't remember much about my mother's illness except she was sick a long time, for years I think now. She was in and out of a hospital somewhere back East a dozen times after our younger brother Bob was born. Because of the expense required for Mama's care, Pa had to sell his first livery and blacksmith business. He needed the money to pay the bank for all the times he'd had to send Mama back east on the train. Then Mama died, and Bob and Jill and I went off to Trinity County once more while Pa and my older brother Carl stayed behind in Comanche where Pa had recently opened up a new blacksmith shop on the southwest corner of the square just across from the bank. The Trinity County arrangement was supposed to last only a short time until Pa could get back on his feet again. Then he intended to send for us kids, but Mama's death changed him. He was never his old self again. A little over a year later he also took sick and died, and Carl took over the shop, being at the time seventeen and recently married.

For the next ten years, before I came back to Comanche County to stay, my life was rather unsettled. I lived one place and then another, although at first I probably spent more time with Wes and his family than with anyone else. Wes had two brothers, Joe and Jeff, and a sister, Mat, and at the time a Negro cook and field hand named Julie Ola Faye, who was the prettiest woman I have ever seen, even if she was a Negro. She had helped raise Wes and was like a second mother to him. The family had owned her as a young girl before the war. After the war, they encouraged her to get out on her own, but she refused to talk about it. Her own mother was dead and buried on the place where they were then living, and she did not want to go off and leave her mother's grave. Besides, she felt Wes was her responsibility, just as a son would have been. Later on when the trouble started and we were always on the run, it seemed Wes worried as much about Mama Julie as he did about his own mother.

In addition to the family, the Hardin estate included a large assortment of animals of the type common to Texas farms of that day and time. It didn't seem to matter if we were living out on the farm or someplace in town. We always had between one and a dozen of just about every farm animal imaginable, from cats and dogs to cattle and mules. The horses, however, were Wes's favorites, and we boys would hold races out in the pasture and bet to see who had to carry the others' books to school or something small like that. Later, as we got older, the bets got bigger and the horses faster, and we were racing at the track rather than in the pasture. Between us we always had more ready cash than we had time to spend. Sometimes we made more money off a single race than the farmers we lived around could make in a year of working their places from sun up to sun down.

Looking back, I think all that may have been a big part of the trouble. We had too much money, and it had been too easy to get. On top of that, we were too young to have any sense. It was an enjoyable time in my life, to be sure; and at the moment I couldn't see any harm in what we did. But looking back, I see that one thing led to another. We just had too much too soon. If we hadn't had all that money, maybe we wouldn't have gambled and drank the way we did. At least, that's what I've always told myself.

Next to the horses, I guess the dogs were Wes's favorite. Most of them were scar-faced, rangy old coon hounds, but we had one particular dog that I don't guess I'll ever forget. We got up one morning and went outside to find him sitting in the yard as though he had been waiting for us to wake up. He was all white and fluffy and like no dog I had ever seen before. He was bigger too. He must have weighed well over a hundred pounds, perhaps as much as a hundred and twenty-five, and was almost as tall as he was long so that he looked more like a fuzzy white bear than he did a dog.

A lawyer friend of Mr. Hardin's came out one day and told us our new dog was a Great Pyrenees. He said these dogs had first been bred in Europe hundreds of years before to fight bears and wolves away from sheep herds in the Pyrenees Mountains in France and Spain. Our dog looked as though he could do just that. He was as much a bear as any bear I could imagine, and he walked like one too, with a kind of rolling gait that started first in the shoulders and spread on back to his rear. But despite his breeding, he was so gentle no one would ever have guessed he was any kind of fighter. I believe he was the gentlest, most loving dog I have ever known. After we learned what he was, we just called him Bear.

Following my mother's death, I renewed my friendship with Wes at the school house in Sumpter in Trinity County where my sister and I and our cousins were attending school, Bob, of course, being still too young to attend. It was easy to like him back then, and almost everyone did. Since he was a little bigger and older than the rest of us, he kind of looked out for us and kept the school bullies from pushing us around too much and stealing our lunches so we didn't have to go all day without anything to eat.

Wes was smarter than the rest of us, also, and on the playground at noon he won all the games, no matter which ones we played. Many times I would bring a whole sack of marbles to school, and by the end of the day Wes would have won every last one of them, though sooner or later he always gave them back.

Wes was a slender, handsome young man of medium height, and he refused to shave the hair off his upper lip so that already at fourteen he had a rather respectable mustache. He was of light complexion and had soft blue eyes just like his father. They were the softest blue I have ever seen.

Though I did not know it then, that year at Sumpter was to be my last full term of formal schooling. I will always believe it was at Sumpter school that Wes got started down the wrong path. What happened there was the first act of violence of its kind and the beginning of something that could only have ended the way it did, though we couldn't have known that back then. But if I were going to put my finger on the one incident that got Wes started, what happened at that school would have to be it. I think that's when Wes first realized his deep attraction to violence, though I had suspected it much earlier. Maybe it was the taste of it in his mouth or the flushed excitement he felt as the idea raced along in his blood, because with Charley Sloter Wes came alive in a way I had not seen before but a way which I was to see many times in the years ahead.

Jim Stephens

Wes had this girl at Sumpter named Elizabeth, and she and Wes were sweet on each other. Sometimes at noon they would slip off from the school and go down in the woods along the creek. They would take their dinner and wouldn't come back until it was time to go inside again. I could understand why they did it even back then, as young as I was. It was spring, and spring is the best time of the year in Texas. It brings the first warm days of the season when you can pull off the shoes you have worn all winter and walk along in the sand with it warm and cool against your feet at the same time. Your feet are still tender and white from wearing shoes too long, and to be able to pull them off at last and walk in the soft sand is the finest feeling in the world. All around you the trees and grass and spring flowers are starting to green, and the air is still and bright under the new spring sun.

So it was spring, and Wes was in love with Elizabeth. I think I was too, even if I was only eleven. She had the prettiest hair of any girl or woman I have ever seen, and it blew in the wind like willow leaves. When she smiled at me, I thought of the sun and the way a ripe wild plum tastes and feels in my mouth when I eat it.

One day I asked Wes, "What do you and Elizabeth do down there in the woods each day?"

I thought I knew the answer to that, but some of the older boys had put me up to asking because they knew Wes was my friend. Later, I realized they were just using me to get at Wes because they were jealous of him and Elizabeth. They were also jealous of his success on the playground and his ability in the school room, but I was naive enough to think they didn't know what I did about Wes and Elizabeth and only wanted to find out. Secretly, they were probably also hoping he was going to knock my head off for poking into something that was none of my business. They had never liked it that I was Wes's friend, and I knew it. But I was young and didn't see any of the other beyond that. I just went ahead and asked anyway.

"Is it something you have to hide because you are ashamed of it?"

At first, Wes just looked at me without saying anything, as though he was trying to decide what to do. He looked at me for a considerable while, and then he looked around at the others where they were standing off at a distance watching. Finally, he looked back at me.

"Why don't you come on along, Jimmy, and find out."

He wasn't mad or anything, and he knew right off the other boys had put me up to asking.

Next day at noon, Wes and Elizabeth and I went off down in the woods along the creek and sat down on an old log that hung out over the water. First we ate our dinner, and after that we just sat there being warm and comfortable in the sun, watching the fish pop flies and gnats off the top of the water. I took my shoes off and trailed my feet down in the creek, slowly moving them back and forth against the drift of the water. Elizabeth did hers too, and I was feeling good about being there with her and Wes and about the older boys knowing I was there.

After a while, Wes and Elizabeth got up and went over along the bank. I continued to dangle my feet off into the water, and out of the corner of my eye I could see them lying back against a drift of white sand that stretched along the bank on that side of the creek. A tree hung out over the water at that point and hid them from anyone who might be trying to spy on them from back in the woods. When I looked again,

Elizabeth had her head down in Wes's lap and lay there looking up at Wes with her long golden hair spread out like sunshine across his legs and some down on her shoulders.

Without saying anything, Wes reached across and untied the front of Elizabeth's dress and pushed it down onto her shoulders. Then he slowly lifted her large breasts out of the material so they lay round and white in the sun where it came down through the leaves on the tree.

At first I was afraid to look, but I couldn't help myself. Then I knew Wes wanted me to watch. That was the reason he brought me along.

After Wes opened the front of her dress, Elizabeth put her hands on her breasts and squeezed in on them. Then she put her hands under them and lifted them up toward Wes a little.

"Please, Wes," she said, smiling at him.

Wes put his hand out and touched one of Elizabeth's breasts and squeezed it a little the way she had done, rolling it around to get the feel of it in his hand. Then he caught up the second one in his other hand, just rolling them around and bunching them together like twin pillows.

Suddenly, Wes stopped what he was doing and looked across at me.

"Okay, Jimmy," he said, "now you know there is something you can use your hands for other than to hold a gun and something else to put your legs around than the half curve of a horse's back."

Elizabeth was just lying there in Wes's lap with her eyes closed and her hair all spread out like sunshine, and when Wes took his hands away, she put her own back, rolling her breasts around the way she had done at first and squeezing the dark nipples some with her fingers.

It was the most wonderful experience I had ever been a part of, and though Wes and I knew a lot of girls in the years that followed, some of them his and some of them mine, whenever I made love to one of them, in my mind I would always see Elizabeth lying back in Wes's lap, holding her soft pretty breasts, with her golden hair flamed out in the sun.

"You go on back now, Jimmy," Wes said.

I got up and walked on up the bank a ways and sat down. I had managed to calm myself somewhat, but I kept thinking about the sun in Elizabeth's hair and the sun hot on her breasts, and I got excited all over again. Then I got up to go on, but I couldn't help looking back. Wes had Elizabeth down on her back with the front of her dress lifted up, and I could see her long white legs spread out against the white sand. I think Wes knew I was still watching, but he didn't care. He wanted me to see what he was doing.

That experience with Wes and Elizabeth was a good lesson to learn. It had been the right thing to do, the most natural thing in the world to do, and there had been no shame or embarrassment. With Wes there never was. Somehow none of it seemed wrong. Wes had something about him that was special. I have always said it. I don't care what he did or what anybody said about him, he was special. He made me feel that I was important to him and that he needed me. I would have done anything for him and been proud to do it. Several others over the years voiced much the same sentiments—Jim and Manning Clements, Jim Taylor and Bud Dixon, and Bud's brother Tom. I don't know—a whole long list of them if I could just think. They would all have given their lives for him if he had asked them to. Several of them eventually did anyway. Wes just had something special about him, some kind of genius, something you couldn't put your finger on. As I have said, in his own way he was as much an artist as any painter or writer who ever lived. What's more, he was always sharing with me the way he did with Elizabeth: his women, his horses, his home, his money—just everything. It was always that way with him, whether we were making love to the same woman or drinking together in a bar or simply burying the lifeless corpses of a couple of worthless backshooting bushwhackers we had just blasted the hell out of.

Jim Stephens

That's the way it was at Sumpter school until one day Wes and Elizabeth came back from the creek a little earlier than usual, and Wes caught this boy Charley Sloter writing a poem on the wall of the school about this homely girl named Sally Wes had befriended because other students sometimes made fun of her. The poem started like this: "I love Sal and Sal loves mutton," and went on from there to reflect on Sal's personal attractions. Wes had seen all us boys gathered around Charley when he and Elizabeth first came out of the woods, and he must have known what was going on. He and Charley had never gotten along, and it wasn't hard to figure out why. Every boy in the school wanted Elizabeth for his girl.

Wes left Elizabeth there in the edge of the pasture and came up quietly behind us before we knew he was there. He just stood there, reading over the tops of our heads while Charley was writing.

"Now, damn him, let him read that!" Charley said when he finished.

He was laughing when he said it, but then he turned and saw Wes. Watching the blood drain out of Charley's face is what told the rest of us Wes was there behind us.

That day was my introduction to the extreme violence Wes was capable of. Years later, it would remind me of a prairie fire sweeping across the plains, leaving the land behind it blackened and ruined—a scene of carnage and waste. I also had not known before how quick tempered Wes was.

At first, Wes and Charley just glared at each other, with Charley kind of hulking behind a frozen grin he had managed to pull up from somewhere. He was a foot taller than Wes, and he stood there daring Wes to wipe the grin off his face and at the same time hoping he wouldn't try.

In Wes I saw no change at all, no excitement, no anger, no emotion whatever that I could tell, except the blue in his eyes had gone hard and flat When Wes didn't say anything, signs of life began to come back into Charley's face. He thought he had Wes now and that Wes was afraid of him. He began to get cocky, and he wanted everyone to see him back Wes down. By this time, Sally had come up and stood reading the poem. The grin on Charley's face got larger and turned into a laugh.

"Now read that if you can, damn you!" he said. Then he turned to walk off.

"You take that back, Sloter!" Wes said. "You erase that and you apologize!"

"I didn't write that, Hardin," Charley said. "Somebody else did. I was only standing here reading it." He was a little surprised Wes had said anything at all, and the color in his face started to wash out again.

"You're a damn liar," Wes said. He said it flat, without anger, and so quiet it was almost a whisper. But Charley started to shake when he heard it. He had already backed off a little, trying to edge around so he'd have room to run.

"I see that you are a coward, too," Wes said then. "I saw you write that, Sloter. Now you had better apologize to Sally here or I will knock your head off."

I thought they were going to have it out then, and I got around behind Charley so he couldn't back up any further and so Wes could push him across me when I bent over. Then the teacher came out for us, and we had to go back inside the school and start our lessons.

That afternoon in the school room, Charley took out his knife and tried to stab Wes. Wes was reading to himself out of one of our school books, and Charley's plan was to come up behind him and stick the blade of the knife into his neck. That's what one of Charley's friends admitted to us later. Charley sat a few seats behind Wes and a couple of rows over, and I was just to one side of Wes, so neither of us saw Charley come up. He must have had the knife down against his side so that no one else saw it either. The students who did notice him rise and begin to walk toward the front of the room thought he was going outside since the only door was on that end of the building. But Wes had suspected something like that since we came in at noon. He knew Charley to be a coward, and he told me he'd heard him open his knife and then get up so he was ready when Charley came up behind him. The first time Charley made a swipe with the knife, Wes jumped out the opposite side of his desk. Charley did not know Wes was waiting for him, and the move surprised him so much he missed his aim and struck Wes's shoulder instead of hitting him in the neck. The strike didn't even cut through Wes's shirt that much.

Then Charley stepped through the desk and lunged at Wes again.

"Now I will kill you!" he said, "No one can call me a liar and live to say he did it."

Even though Charley was older and bigger, Wes caught Charley's arm and took the knife away from him. When Charley tried to get it back, Wes stabbed him twice, once in his back and once in his chest. The stabs were hard, and Wes pushed the long wide blade of the knife in to the handle both times. The second time he hit something hard so that the blade wouldn't go in all the way. He had to wiggle it free and push it again. This time it went in. By the time Wes pulled the knife free that second time, the wound was so big the blood followed the blade out and began to run through the hole in Charley's shirt.

For a moment Charley stood there looking down at the blood. Then he put his hand through the rip in his shirt and tried to find the big wound so he could put his finger in it and stop the blood. By this time maybe half a cup of blood had spilled out on the floor. Charley still hadn't said anything, but when he found the wound with his finger, he groaned. Then he fell over across one of the seats and then on off onto the floor and just lay there looking up at us.

"Help me, I'm dying!" he said. "Help me, I'm dying!"

"Say you wrote it now!" Wes said to him. "Admit you wrote it or I will kill you for sure!"

The girls were screaming and running out of the school room, and the teacher was trying to talk Wes into putting the knife down. But Wes wasn't threatening Charley now. He was just standing over him, watching him bleed. His attention had shifted to the spectacle, and he wasn't mad anymore. The bleeding was just something to be amazed at and to wonder about. And in no way did Wes's behavior seem very wrong. None of us standing around could think of anything else he could have done. We would have taken the same action if we had been in his place and could have found the courage. It had been the only action to take and the right action, also, and it would seem that way with every thing Wes did after that until he went to prison. It was just the idea of what Wes was doing that people didn't like, not the wrongness of his intentions or even Wes himself but the idea behind it all. And it was the idea finally that got him tried, convicted, and incarcerated in the state penitentiary at Huntsville.

After a few minutes men came to the school and took the knife away from Wes and carried Charley to the doctor. At first, we didn't know how bad he was hurt, but later we were told he almost died lying there on the school room floor. When people found that out, they got mad. They were worried about their kids, and they wanted Wes removed from the school. But Wes had too many friends for that, and the incident hadn't been his fault. Even the school trustees and later the county judge could see the truth. It didn't matter, though. School was never the same again. Elizabeth's family sent her off to another school, and Charley never came back either. All Wes ever said was, "That bastard, that damned cowardly bastard. He deserved to die. He asked to die."

Wes wasn't mad when he said it, but he wasn't sorry either about what he had done to Charley. I can't explain it, but it was as though Wes thought people could by some foolish act or word give up their right to live. Once they had done that, they didn't count as people anymore and weren't worth his consideration. I don't know how accurate that explanation is, but Wes was right about Charley Sloter. A couple of years later we heard he got himself hanged by a mob over in the next county for trying to rob a bank.

Julie Ola Faye

Shooooeeee, but aint hit hot. Hits so hot I thinks I is gonna turn into muddy water and run off down dese rows till I sink under de sand. Sometime dere is nothin worse dan dis heat. When you hasta works out in de field like dis, hit jest iches you and gits in yo mouth till you caint do no work at all. Laudy, dis sand is so hot on yo feet you thinks you is walkin thru a skillet of boilin grease where de fatback is fryin and de sweat is rollin off you and you is dancin neckid in de fire with John Wesley Hardin. One of you is a murderer and de other is a whore. Oh my son my son, de great mother of Babylon is burnin in de fire, burnin in de white sand of sin.

If hit was jest me and dis ole dog. If it was not him and dis boy, I would pull off my dress and let dat wind blow cool, oh laudy, thru my parts like pears hangin heavy from de tree. Like ripe golden pears waitin to be picked and bit and sucked and chewed and et, hangin loose on de tree blowin cool in de wind at night. So cool, so wet and so cool.

Sometime I has thoughts. I dont mean my visions of de chariot dat runs in de streets wid out mules. De chariot dat burns wid fire to hunt down John Wesley and kill him. But thoughts bout dese two fat-nippled breasts mens caint keep dey hands off of. White mens or black mens neither. Dey mouths off of neither. De way dey hang down when I bends over like pears in de wind. If dey jest had hands you ole colored woman, jest look how much cotton you could pull. If dey was hands hangin down dere like dat catchin on de tops of de stalks. Or think how good four hands would be now helpin to pull out dis ole goose grass from dese little bitty ole cotton plants.

"Yank up dere, you two ole breasts you. Yank up dat goose grass by de neck."

Den dey would be good for somethin sides mens hands and dey mouths.

But I swear Id do hit. Cause dogs aint people. I would jest pull everthing off. If de Laud dont like to look on all dis colored nigger flesh, den he can turn round and look de other way. I jest stand right up here like my mama dropped me out of her belly and lets de wind blow cool. Laudy, whats will I do when hit really gits hot?"

Now hit was hot back den when I was young too. Papa say, "You close dat window fore you go to sleep, girl."

"Hits too hot, Papa," I says.

Papa's cousin, he come to me and me only fourteen.

"I aint asked yo pa yet," he say, "but I is lookin for me a good woman right now."

He was bout twenty. Papa say to me, "Girl, you marry a nigger dat is good and dark, not one of dem creamy niggers dat is all washed out."

Jest fore my sister sold, Papa's cousin say to Papa, "I wants to marry your daughter, Julie Ola Faye."

"You is a no count, lazy nigger," Papa say. "I never did want no such lazy nigger, even for a cousin. Specially no washed out, creamy nigger."

Dat night Papa say, "Girl, you close dat window."

"Hits too hot in dis room, Papa," I says. "Hits too hot even for dogs to sleep."

Masta Johnny say we gots to finish today fore supper time.

"I got to go into Comanche and buy John Wesley a drink on his birthday like I told him I would," he say.

He git mad cause I wont say *James* like his name is. But I wont. I dont like it. Never did. Hits jest *Johnny* to me. Masta Johnny.

Oh laudy, dat child. Dat John Wesley.

So I can quit by supper time too, dis child and me and dis ole white dog, and goes home and kills de fatted hog like Masta wants, though I told him hits too hot for no hog killin.

Dis sweat, so cool. Oh laudy, such thoughts as go thru dis ole niggers head. Thoughts of de men and der hands. Mama say to me, "Girl child, not even Jesus can save you. You looks like a whore and you acts like a whore."

Oh, Sweet Jesus, forgive me. Sometimes I think if Masta Johnny was jest not a preacher, den I could say to him, *"Laudy, Masta Johnny, I have sinned. Even by not sinnin I have sinned."*

What smoke dat is! How big and tall and dark! Hits like a nigger standin up aginst de clouds wid out no clothes on. What mean smoke dat is. Dat John Wesley agin. He done burned up de whole town and killed all de people.

Masta Johnny say quit by supper. Den he say, "You have got to kill that hog."

"But hits too hot for no killin. Hit will spoil jest like you planted dis cotton too early and hits already up and needin to be chopped. By June hit will ruin jest like dat ole hog will ruin."

"It is all we are gonna have to eat," he says. "There aint likely to be another week so cool as this one. Besides, its leg is broke."

And me wid dis sweat. Sometime I could jest pull off dis dress. If hit was jest me and dis ole white dog. I swear dat smoke look jest like a nigger. Dat John Wesley. I love dat boy. I love him jest like he was my own son. He says "Mama Julie, I have killed a man."

"Oh my son, my son!"

"He is a nigger like yourself named Mage. Barnett Jones and I beat him wrestling, and I had to kill him."

"And you only a boy, my son."

"We scratched his face, Mama Julie Ola Faye. He said he would kill me or die himself. He said no white boy could draw his blood and live, Mama Julie. He said a bird never flew too high not to come to the ground."

"Oh my son!"

By 1869 he kill three more. Three soldiers, one of em a nigger.

"Mama Julie Ola Faye, I buried them in a creek. They came after me, Mama Julie."

And him not de least bit sorry.

"They wanted to kill me. They didn't have no cause. They just heard about me and wanted to be the ones to kill me."

And me lovin dat boy jest like he was my own.

"I got two of them with my shotgun, Mama Julie."

Oh laudy, hits so hot. I wished I was dat ole smoke standin up dere in de clouds for de whole world to see, lettin de wind blow cool thru my parts, lettin de hands of de Laud feel on dese ole breasts.

"Shame on you, girl child," my mama used to say. "Hits dat bad blood talkin to you. Hits ole willy nilly Whitey's blood in you, child. Hits done mixed wid yo colored blood and you is a lost soul."

Oh laudy, so hot. Shooooeeee, dese tits. Dese breasts. If dey was jest hands, I could pick me two bales a day wid time off for de shade. Dey has such a shape, such a feel to em. Dey caint stay out of mens hands. White mens or black mens. Dey wont stay out of even preachers hands.

"Hits dat bad blood," Mama say. "Bad blood makin em like dey is."

Dey is bad tits like Mama say. Always pokin out dere seein what dere is to see. Sayin, "Dere is a man to hold us wid, Honey. One wid hands to make us feel oh so good."

Shame! Shame on you, you ole black nigger whore you! Jesus Christ will think you is a whore for sho, and he will strike you dead like lightnin out of a tornado. You will be here and den you wont be here. *"Where did dat poor ole nigger woman go?"* folks will say. *"Where did she go?"*

If dey wouldnt jest go pokin out dere tryin to see like dey had eyes and was people. So Mama took me to be saved by de preacher and den he preached. He say, "My friends, dis here been a good day and we is all so happy to be here on dis day.

God has worked miracles in front of us dis day. He has taken
dis here girl wid de bad blood and brought her to me and we
went up to de house yonder and prayed bout her bad blood
and de Laud cured her. He sholy did. Praise de Laud. Yes,
Jesus."

And preached he did. "Amen, Brother! Amen! Amen!" And
wid his smell still all over me and de prints of his hands still
on my tits where he squeezed em so hard and his sweat mixed
wid my sweat and my bottom sore where his ole horse dong
punched on me and run out on me like soured syrup.

"Oh tell us bout it, Preacher! Amen!"

"Yes, Jesus, my friends. Nother soul been struck down on
de road to Demascus. Nother child of de Laud been raised up
in her place. Oh Laud, we thank you for yo bountiful love."

By now he was shoutin and jumpin round and dey was
sayin "Preach hit, Brother, preach hit! Oh yes, Jesus come
quick! Come Holy Spirit!"

And de smell of him still all over me like soured syrup in
de jug. If Masta Johnny was jest not a preacher wrapped up
like dat in dem black clothes wid dat Bible tied up round his
middle wid a rope, den I could say to him, *"Laud, I have sinned
and is in need of forgiveness. John Wesley needs it too, ole
Masta Johnny. Laud forgive John Wesley and forgive dis ole
nigger whore too."*

Dere dat smoke agin. John Wesley done set de whole town
on fire. Dat boy! And when I was jest twenty or so and him
jest born, I would pick him up in my arms and let down de
front of my dress and from one side I would suckle de white
one and from de other side I would suckly mine own dark one.
Laudy, he lay dere so quiet. Maybe God had two sons by de
Virgin Mary. A black one and a white one. And de black one
took de colic and died and de white one he named J.W. Jesus.
Oh laudy, I was so proud of dem two men childs. I thought
dey was such fine ones to have. But Mama say to me, "You is
too proud, child. Specially you is too proud for no whore. Hits
dat bad blood in you. Jesus Christ will make you sorry for
your pride. Jest you wait and see."

And I guess my mama was right, bless her poor ole lost sweet mama's soul. Cause one day when he was jest fifteen, de law come and got my dark one and carried him off. "For jest a year," dey say. "We will keep him jest one year, Julie Ola Faye, and then you can have him back."

But hits been six years now, and we dont even know where he is for sho and jest cause he took dat whiskey out of dat store cause he was thirsty. Oh laudy, sometimes I jest wants to lie back in de bed at night and pray to de Laud for rain. I jest want to lie still and quiet in de dark waitin for hit to come. Smellin hit first and den hearin hit pound on dat ole piece of tin where I hads to crawl up and patch de roof. Sometimes I thinks hits de sweetest sound I ever heard. I jest wants to lie back wid nothin but de sheet coverin me and listen to de stories hits tellin bout my visions and bout my sins and bout my dark lost mama.

We had us a ole preacher once who say all us ole nigger whores was decended from Lilith.

"Who is dat Lilith, Preacher?" I says.

"Adam's first wife," he say. "Mother of all old nigger whores."

If Masta Johnny was jest not a preacher, I would go to him neckid in my sin. But oh dat John Wesley. My son, my son. So much like my own flesh and blood hits like he was my second one and him up dere in Comanche now racin dem horses. Ole Rondo dat he got off dat Ansley farmer live jest north of us. Racin dem horses and shootin off dem guns.

"Mama Julie," he come to me when hit was de first one, "Mama Julie Ola Faye, you are the only nigger I have ever trusted. If I did not have a real mother, I would want you to be my mother. My sweet old colored mother."

"I knows, boy," I says.

"Mama Julie, I have just killed a man. See, this old .44 six-shooter, and he was a nigger like you. He was a big black arrogant nigger, and he wouldn't get out of the middle of the road, so I shot him down. I killed him where he stood with this very gun."

"Oh Laudy, Johnny Boy! Oh my poor sweet John Wesley, and you jest a boy yet."

"He hit me with his stick, Mama Julie."

Cept even back den, it was already dem guns and bettin on anything and everything from horses to dogs to chickens to who could pick de most cotton. My how he would fight me at de tit after he got growed some.

"You aint got no call to bite at me like dat, you young white devil."

And him not even a year old, pushin and fightin at my tit like dat wid my dark one lyin on de other side as quiet and peaceful as you please.

"Dat J.W. Jesus boy will break womens hearts when he is older," Mama said.

But Mama didnt mean wid no gun. She meant by lovin dem and leavin dem, and him fightin my tit like dat and him only a baby. And by 1869 hit was four. Now dey is sayin hits almost forty. Oh laudy, four by 1869 and now dey is saying over thirty more and how he cuts each one into dat willow stick he carry in his pocket. Now Masta Johnny dont ever go no where wid out dat shotgun in de wagon. Poor John Wesley and his father a preacher and him wid dat fancy preachers name, kickin and buckin at de tit like a wild goat, hunchin up at me.

Poor John Wesley. So now he has done gone and burned down de whole town and maybe hisself wid it. Breakin womens hearts by killin der husbands and sons. And wid dat name after de fancy preacher, bitin and kickin and hunchin up at de tit even when he was a baby.

"Mama Julie, I killed that third one, that nigger soldier, with my pistol."

Oh Sweet Jesus, come quick. One ole nigger whore caint save de world by herself. She aint got no cross to die on and she needs all de blood she got jest to live. She caint spare none to give away. Dere jest aint enough for folks to wash in. She jest caint. She gots to save em wid love. She gots plenty of dat for sho.

And me lovin John Wesley and like a mother layin wake nights worryin bout him and dreamin my visions bout him and him not de least bit sorry for what he done.

What's he gonna say to me now? *"Mama Julie, I have just burned down the town of Comanche and hanged all the people because they didn't like me and wouldn't get out of the middle of the street."*

Oh laudy, dat smoke is jest worse and worse and soon dey will be comin after me, sayin, *"Where have you hid him? Where is your white son J.W. Jesus?"*

Oh laudy, I wished I was where ole nigger whores go when dey aint no count no more, but further dan de woods cause my boy hid out dere when he took dat whiskey. When he didnt come home, I went out and got him.

"What you doing crouchin down behind dat bush, boy. Has you done somethin to hide for?"

"Mama Julie, I has committed sin."

Dat smoke is comin. I know hit is. If hit was jest me and dis ole white dog, I would go where ole useless niggers go. Where ole whores and dere murderin sons go. Comin now thru de woods. I can see hit comin sho nuff.

My son, de murderer of men, and each one he kill since den is cut into dat stick and is a knife in my heart. Each one a lifetime. Each one de days and minutes hit took de Laud to build dis ole world of death and sin. Oh sweet Mama alone in de rain at night, tellin de ole wild tales of regret and sadness.

"Kill it by supper," Masta Johnny say, "so it can hang overnight in the smokehouse."

"Hits too late in de spring. Hit will never keep," I says.

"We aint got no choice," he say. "It won't give you no fight with that broke leg. First you start that pot boiling and then you take out that gun."

"But a sticks better," I says. "I have always used me a big stick, and dey aint never give me no trouble dat way."

"You use that gun," he say.

Shoooeeeee, dis sweat. Dis ole dress is jest wet. Dat sweat blowin cool in de wind, and hit was like dat when I was young and my first masta come up to me in de field.

"Julie Ola Faye," he say, "you are the prettiest young nigger I have ever seen."

I had on an ole dress den jest like dis one and I was only fifteen, but dese breasts was already leanin out der lookin round.

"You are, to be sure, the prettiest nigger," he say.

"Thank you, Masta," I says.

Cause Mama say he would be comin after me sooner or later.

"You caint stop em when you are so pretty as dat," she say. "Dey will come for you and dey will spect you to do what dey says."

Dat was fore dey started killin one another in de war somewheres up north. Somewhere I can hear glass breakin. Hit has been breakin since I got in de field dis mornin. My J.W. Jesus boy say to me, *Mama Julie Ola Faye, when I die I will shatter all glass everywhere. It will break out in mourning for my passing and fall out in the streets.*

Dat smoke is comin. I see it yonder in de woods. Hits comin fast.

"Masta Johnny!"

Jim Stephens

Sitting on the train listening to those cultured and polished gentlemen muse on life in the Comanche County of Texas immediately after the war and in the Reconstruction years that followed was a journey into the past. It was a pilgrimage I would have preferred not to start and certainly not alone, but the past is curiously attractive and strangely compelling. Sometimes, willingly or otherwise, we do go back, each in his own way and each for his own reasons. For most, the past is pleasantly vague and stands in relationship to the present only as reference. For a tortured few, its reality is so close and intense that five, ten or even twenty years are as yesterday and their joys and fears and victories and losses and their great sadnesses only a short sleep away. It's as though time has borne them on its swelling flood almost no distance so that they can still see the place where they first stepped into its moving flow.

It was like that on the train that day. It was the present, and I was coming home from a lengthy visit. Suddenly it was yesterday once more. I was a boy again, remembering a friend that I had loved and a time whose images as I relived them were quick and poignant with only the brief night of sleep between any of it and the present moment. I was back in school again, and Wes was there. Charley Sloter had been knifed and had recovered, and Elizabeth was gone. Wes and I were closer than ever and were spending more time together, especially away from Sumpter school. What we had shared with Elizabeth, no matter how small my part, became a bond between us, and my sympathy and loyalty to Wes when he had almost killed Charley was but a strengthening of that bond.

It wasn't long after Elizabeth left that Wes and I became inseparable. I had a fine bay horse that Wes had picked out for me and bought with money we both had earned doing whatever jobs we could find to do. It was almost as good a horse as the one he rode. After I grew familiar with it, we would ride into the neighboring towns around Sumpter, starting early in the morning before the sun was up. Once we reached a town, we would water and stable the horses and then find a place on the board walk where we could watch what was going on in town. We especially liked to sit outside the saloons and watch people coming and going. We were always hoping we would get to see a fight, and on several occasions we did. But it wasn't just that. It was the old men too and the tales they told and the women in their fine clothes and their white starched bonnets and the young girls who followed them and could not keep from turning back and looking at Wes as they moved on down the street. He was handsome almost beyond measure and had a swagger about him. Even leaning back against a building, half in shadow, with only his worn, tattered boots and long thin legs catching any sun at all, he still had that swagger. It was interesting to watch—the way people came up to him, the way they were drawn to him. I envied him that appeal, but more strongly I felt honored he had picked me as a friend.

Sometimes while we were standing around, Wes would talk to me about the cowboys who came by and the kinds of guns they wore on their belts. He liked to speculate about which ones could use their guns and which ones just wore them because carrying a gun made them feel important. Most, of course, were farmers whose guns were like their hoes or plows to them. A gun was a tool only, and they used it as a tool—not quick or fancy but efficiently. When the need for it passed, they would lay it aside just as they would any other tool and not pick it up again until the next time they needed it.

Still others put great stock in their guns, both in how they wore them and in their ability to use them. To be able to handle a gun well was important to them, and they wanted it known that they had that skill. It was these men who interested Wes. He was a remarkable judge of character and motive, and gradually I began to pick up some of the reasoning he used in making judgments. I do not doubt that it was this ability, more than it was his skill with guns, that kept him alive long enough to be tried and sent to jail.

Wes always knew what another man was thinking and what he was likely to do. In many cases I am persuaded he knew even before the man knew himself. I never became that good, but I did learn some of what to look for. I learned to watch the way a man acted and how he moved his hands. I learned to listen to what he said and to weigh his reasons for saying it. Wes always said people were like books in that respect. They had to be studied and read. He said the way they walked and used their hands were like illustrations in a book and made the reading easier to understand. It was as though the book said to you, "On the following page this man is going to take out his gun and shoot you. He is thinking of doing it on this page and on the next page he will surely do it." Wes said if you were reading carefully you always had time to take out your own gun and have it ready while the page was being turned.

As I mentioned, Wes and I did see several fights visiting the small towns around Sumpter, though nothing spectacular. Most were between drunks, with the result being broken noses and hands and occasionally someone being hauled off to jail. Once in one of the towns, a stray bullet broke out the window of the bank, and for a few minutes people inside thought the bank was under attack. Similar incidents made up our daily fare, with nothing much beyond that for excitement. It was the different kinds of people—their shapes and personalities, their ways of walking and of carrying themselves—that proved finally to be of most interest. Strangely enough, it's the kind of detail you never see unless you sit down and slow your mind enough to take notice. And a good deal of what we observed was humorous. It's amazing what you can figure out about people you don't know, if you will just observe them closely enough. Several times we rode home with our sides sore from having laughed so much at the oddities we had discovered.

Going back home at night was, by the way, another story. For all his intelligence and bravado, Wes was strangely superstitious. His constant association with Negroes while he was growing up had given him a mortal fear concerning ghosts and spirits and graveyards and dead men's bones and the like. Many was the time he thought he saw a ghost, and his fear was so real that sometimes I believed I had seen one too. Looking back, I realize that I wanted to see one just because Wes had. To the terror of the moment, we could both add horrifying details to what had started out as the simplest of occurrences with the simplest of explanations—a strange cry in the woods, an unfamiliar noise, a light suddenly gleaming out of nothing and then gone. Even upon reaching home, we would sometimes lie in bed, afraid even to breathe, until sheer tension and exhaustion put us to sleep.

Curiously enough, it was way back in '61, in Sumpter itself, where Wes and I got that first taste of excitement and danger that would serve as a pattern for much of what happened to us in later years. On this particular occasion, Wes and I saw our first man killed, and it was almost by accident we were present at all. Mr. Hardin was going in to Sumpter that day for supplies. Being a Saturday with no school and nothing else in particular to do that day, Wes and I hitched a ride in on the wagon. Ordinarily, we would have been out somewhere riding horses, but Wes's horse had a sore foot and the old nag I rode at the time was clear to the other side of the pasture.

"Jimmy, why don't we go into town with Pa?" Wes asked.

So we did, and what we witnessed there gave us something to muse about for weeks to come. It was exactly the kind of incident that the gentlemen sitting with me in the smoker had in mind about Texas in general and the town of Comanche in particular. To be fair, a good deal did happen in Comanche and the surrounding county in the thirty years or so after the ending of the war, though a similar statement could be made as easily about a dozen other counties. I am thinking in particular not just of the several years we lived with the threat of Indian violence or of the fabled exploits of my friend Wes Hardin. I also have in mind the fancy-dressing, fancy-talking Negro who killed Ben Stephens's young wife, and for the trouble got himself hanged and his bones put in a jar to be sold off as curiosities, with the added result of the rest of the Negroes being run out of the county and a sign put up warning them not to return. I am thinking too of Mavis Ansley, who sold Wes Old Rondo, Wes's famous race horse, and of the famous fence responsible for Ansley's death. A half dozen other incidents might be mentioned as well, all in part responsible for the notoriety of Comanche County. But much good might be noted also, though the gentlemen on the train would never hear about that. Myths and legends die hard. It is change and progress people forget about. Nevertheless, my gentlemen friends on the train would have enjoyed being with Wes and me in Sumpter the day Old John Ruff killed Turner Evans.

Turner Evans and Old John Ruff were a strange pairing. Collusion of almost any kind requires at the outset at least some natural sympathies, whether external or otherwise, although collusion in violence less frequently so. Still, that these particular two men could ever have—well, it was most amazing. Old John Ruff was a poor man and had been all his life. As far as I knew, he was also a good and honest man and, if unprovoked, a nonviolent one. Though he was in his seventies, he still worked and farmed his land, supporting himself and his wife as well as his only child, who had never left home, and her illegitimate offspring. Even at his age he rose at four o'clock each morning as he had done all of his life, beginning as a child. He went first to the barn and milked five cows and fed half a dozen others and then strained the milk and set it out to cool so that his wife could begin the preparations necessary to turn it into butter and cheese, which later he would take into town to peddle. After finishing with the cows, he would walk the two miles to the creek and there check his fishing lines, take the catch off, and rebait. Carrying the string of fish home, he would clean them, clean and dress himself, and by sunup be ready to sit down to the hot breakfast of biscuits and pork and eggs and homemade syrup his wife had been up since five preparing.

The daughter, an idiot in her forties at the time of the fight, had some years before managed to attract a whole string of men, despite the state of her mind. One of these men got her with child, and then left the country, with Old John and his wife none the wiser. One day she came walking in from the cow lot carrying the naked, screaming child in her arms. After giving birth to it on the hay, she had tried to feed it in the hog trough, and it had slop all over its face. She carried it into the house slung down over one arm as though it might have been a new puppy. She had always been a big eater, and all that time she was carrying the child Old John and his wife thought she was only getting fat. They never suspected her real condition.

The man had most likely been a hired hand who had helped out for about six weeks one spring after Old John came down with the flu and later pneumonia. He left one morning without giving notice or coming by to collect his last week's pay. The first the Ruffs knew of his departure was the cows bawling in the barn late that morning because they had not been fed. Prior to coming to Texas and working for Old John, the man had lived for several years in Mississippi, and as soon as Old John saw the child he was determined to go there and either bring the man back to marry his daughter or kill him where he stood and be done with it. He even went so far as to pack a small bag and buy himself a gun.

It was the sheriff who had to come out at last and tell Old John and his wife the sad facts about their daughter. Although a dozen others could have supplied full details, he was the logical choice. Apparently the daughter had never been as disadvantaged or as unattractive to men as one would have supposed her condition to suggest. For years, like her father, she had also risen at four, not to do her chores but to go into the woods to meet with first one and then another of the neighboring farm boys. During the day she used the barn, receiving her visitors there as other women might guests in a parlor. Sometimes, the sheriff told Old John, she might have two or three waiting.

This enlightenment sobered Old John, and after whipping the girl with a harness strap, he chained her to her bed, turning her loose only when he had time to keep his eye on her.

Outside of that one incident, Old John's life had been pretty much like anyone else's, and even the granddaughter turned out to be a comfort to him in his old age. He and his wife raised her as their own child, and by the time she was three she was riding into town in the wagon with her grandfather to deliver the milk, butter and cheese. Perched upon the seat like an overgrown blond puppy or perhaps like a miniature woman, she would tell her grandfather to watch what he was doing and not to cuss at the mules and to slow down, just as she had seen her grandmother do—and she just as normal as you please, despite what her mother was.

Turner Evans, now, was just the opposite of Old John. He was a younger man, quite rich, and as arrogant about that last as you could ever imagine. While it would never have occurred to Old John that the accident of his birth carried with it any special license to treat other men as scum, Turner Evans regarded such behavior as his birthright. It seems that Old John had run into financial difficulty some time before and had borrowed money from Evans, resulting in a mortgage on the place he farmed. For years Evans had been upping the ante on the mortgage, not only by requiring larger and larger portions of Old John's crops each fall but also by telling around that Old John was negligent on his debt and in other ways a scoundrel.

Not a man quick to anger, except when pushed too far—a point beyond where other men would have taken up the gun or ax—Old John was resolved to carry his burden as best he could.

"Mary," he had told his wife, "we obviously made a second mistake or have compounded on that first mistake and are now getting some of the interest back."

Sometime early in the afternoon of the day in question, Evans began to drink, and being rich and influential soon had a crowd of ten or so hangers-on around him as he made his way around town looking for Old John. He'd heard Old John was in town and was determined to confront him about the law. Wes and I knew nothing of this at the time, but it just so happened that we were sitting in a small grocery store down on one end of the street listening to Old John and a couple of other men talk about horses. Eventually, Evans made his way to the grocery store. He had always been a large man and fairly imposing in his bearing. Now, fired with drink and disheveled in both appearance and manner, he appeared like a prophet of old just returned from years of desert wandering. His hair was wind tossed and his eyes burning with misplaced indignation. To complete the picture, he carried a large hand-made cane, so thick along its length it was not so much walking stick as club.

As soon as Evans spotted his quarry, he started in to berate Old John. Old John, on the other hand, just sat there in his chair not moving, hoping his accuser would finish and leave him alone. But Evans was more than a little drunk, and with such a number of his followers watching, he would not back away. Besides, Old John did not seem a threat. He was old and so thin his clothes appeared always to be sliding off his body for lack of any meat to hold them on. Perhaps it was this seeming defenselessness that suspended what little sense Evans was reputed to have. He stood in front of Old John, calling him every low-down name I had ever heard and doing it with a strange drunken eloquence. Finally, Old John took all he could and stood up beside his chair.

"Turner, you have ruined me financially and now come with your crowd to attack me personally. Go off!"

With that, Old John tried to leave, but Evans was standing in the front door, blocking it off, and his followers were crowded up around him so thick they couldn't have moved quickly if they'd had wanted to. Seeing this, Old John turned back to Evans.

"Go off!" he said.

"I will, after I have caned you!" Evans said.

Having said this, he began to hit Old John over the head with the thinner end of his cane. Even though it was slender down at the business end despite its thickness otherwise, it was more than adequate as a rod to beat on Old John, with the effect that he seemed to shrink with each blow. At first, Ruff was as surprised as any of us and tried to back away, but the interior of the store was small and he had nowhere to go. Though he had backed as far as he could, he refused to defend himself other than to throw up his hands.

Old John might have continued to let Evans hit at him had Evans not started in about Old John's daughter and her illegitimate child. That addition Old John refused to take. He rose suddenly to full height, and from beneath his belt, with a quickness and skill I would not have credited him with, he pulled a large Bowie knife and began to advance on Turner Evans. His character changed also. He was no longer old, hobbled, stooped John Ruff but a different man. If I had just approached the scene and someone had said to me, "That fellow with the knife is a famous mountain man who singlehandedly drove the grizzlies and Indians out of the Rocky Mountains," I would have replied, "Yes, I can well believe it." From where I stood Old John was a formidable sight and must have been even more so to Turner Evans.

At this point some of Evans's followers stepped forward to prevent Old John—an act which seemed to require nothing more than simple implementation and reasonable care. This was not the case. Old John had gone wild, and no one could get close to him. He swung the long, heavy knife like a battle ax, and he broke up or cut through everything Evans's followers stuck in front of him. Evans, meanwhile, continued to defend himself with the cane, but every time he swung it, Old John cut off another six inches or so until there was neither any cane left to hit with nor space to back into. Those who at first had thought to stop Old John now took thought for their lives.

The strangest fact, to me, about any of what was going on was Wes's response. He stood against one wall transfixed, his eyes dished out like milk saucers as if he were trying to hold in all he was seeing and just barely could. His face was beaming with the experience in the way some men are affected by money and others by women.

By now, Old John had backed Evans into a corner and was slicing him down as he earlier had done the cane. Evans was leaning against the wall for support, watching with a kind of childlike wonder and horror as the knife ripped into his clothes and dug wide ugly trenches along his stomach and chest. At last Old John brought the knife diagonally across Evans's neck and immediately he slumped to the floor with the blood bubbling out of his jugular. In another minute it was over, and Evans was dead.

Old John's attack on Turner Evans had been a frightening event to witness, especially seeing the horror in Evans's eyes once he realized he was going to die no matter what he did to try and prevent it. Going home that afternoon, Wes characterized what we had seen as "damn fine!" At the time I thought Wes's statement harsh and unfeeling, but looking back on this incident in later years I came to see that his excitement lay not in seeing Evans die but in being close enough to death to study it.

Anonymous

The man stood rooted to the spot where he had first stepped down from the wagon upon seeing the horse and its rider come out of the woods. He stood unmoving as if the nimble leap from the wagon's seat had carried with it sufficient force and weight to bury him some inches into the ground, so like the Colossus of old he now stood unyielding.

But this man was no Colossus. He was James Gibson Hardin, circuit riding Methodist preacher, itinerant farmer and sometimes lawyer and schoolteacher. No one had ever yet accused him of the slightest inactivity and certainly not immobility. It would never have occurred to them to do so. Behind him on the wagon seat, the worn ancient Bible lay open, its fine linen pages turning occasionally in the soft-fingered wind.

The Reverend Hardin stood thus now, his finely molded yet muscular hands, as suited to the handle of an ax as to the spine of a Bible, clinched tightly into the pockets of his coat as though he might be trying to push himself on down into the sand and disappear. Actually, he stood frozen as much from concentration as from fear, his eyes never for a moment leaving the oncoming figure which moved steadily forward, not so much running now as floating, dream-like. And as the Reverend Hardin watched, he thought, *Here comes that past again, that hungry past which keeps eating up my present and that of my family until for over five years now we have had no future to speak of—not even enough future to say, "Now I will go out and buy me some new cotton sacks so I can be ready in the fall to pick what I planted in the spring." It is like riding down the creek on the crest of a headrise. Whoever said the past is past and remains in the past is a liar, and God hates a liar. I have read that. Whoever said each day is a new day with new opportunities was a liar, too, and maybe the same liar, I don't know. What I do know is that the past is exactly a headrise, a flood from the past, and it is all I can do to keep one step ahead of it, much less stay long enough in one place to pick the cotton I have planted.*

But wait. The Lord said to have faith and be of a stout heart. Perhaps it is not me the rider wants. Not me he wants to see and talk to. What I ought to do right now is pick up my hoe and start down another row.

But still the Reverend Hardin stood unmoving, his fear growing and apprehension beading in tiny drops of sweat along the sharp lines of his face, his mind racing on ahead, thinking, *If let there be love, then why THIS? Why this horribleness that for lack of a better word we call the past? If love, then why THIS that is yet to come?*

Behind him in the crawling wind, the fine linen pages wherein he had tried earlier to find an answer to his question seemed to laugh at him, and before him the horse and rider came on, dream-like, proportional, drawn along the quick, sharp line of his own urgent need for the matter not to concern him or even to interest him. Though he knew he could not, he would have liked to be able to say to the Negro woman, "What Horse? What Rider?" even as he would like to have said "What smoke?" Instead he continued to study the rider, and he thought, *Yes, pulled along a string whose far end is tied somewhere close to that fire and whose near end is tied to me, though I did not care enough at first even to ride over there and see what was causing all the smoke. But I was wrong. It didn't need either wind or time, not when it could find someone to gather it up in a bucket and bring it four miles on a horse to where I am trying to work and occasionally to read. No, certainly not! It's as though the fire said, "All right, who wants to be the recipient of this action and partially the cause of it?"*

And I, proud fool that I am, could not be content to let it pick someone who was already there in town, someone whose accessibility and proximity would not have required feats of magic such as manipulating four miles of uneven ground, on through woods and sand, not to mention a wind blowing from the wrong direction.

"Here, pick me," I probably said. And maybe I was just tempting it because I believed that no fire could come four miles against the wind and cross one stretch of woods and another of sand.

"Here, take me," I must have said. "I have not had enough trouble in my life. I have not moved often enough and fought battles enough and been poor and gone hungry enough or carried a shotgun around half cocked enough. So here, take me and let me know as soon as you can what prize I will receive for volunteering like this. I need to know in what direction to run and how fast."

Above him in the air, in the dread past of his mind, the Reverend Hardin saw again the old violence brought now to the front by mounting fear and apprehension. A loyal Texan and Confederate at the beginning of the war, he had, nevertheless, been persuaded by his friends not to accompany them when their newly-formed company left for Richmond, even though at first they had elected him captain. Despite that distancing, he remembered, as if they were his own, the stories these same friends told on their return of the nights and years during the war, huddled close around niggard fires, trying to hold in the warmth while absorbing the light—nights when even the smallest of fires was dangerous. Years later and a thousand miles farther west, he had taken the same care just because his name was Hardin and he had a son he'd been arrogant enough to name after a famous English preacher. Indeed, on many a night he had huddled under a tarp in the cold rain just to keep his neck and those of his wife and children out of a noose, thinking to himself what a fool he had been to imagine, despite the end of the war, that anything was ever over or finished.

And in 1865, in Sumpter, Texas, the Reverend Hardin had thought just that, having said, *Now we are done with that forever. It is finished, and we have all had enough of terror and death. We walked into the face of that terror, into the grinning death, and now it is over. We have put down our rifles and unbuckled our swords, and there in the midst of the dust and blood and proud death of that last battlefield whose name we cannot even remember, we pulled off the grey, sweat-soaked, fear-soaked rotted uniforms they issued us three years before and hung them over a limb. From a pack tied on our saddles, we took out the hat and shirt and britches we had worn on the day we enlisted and put them on and turned our horses' heads back to Texas. In our pockets as we rode, we fingered the brass buttons we had torn from the disintegrating cloth of our uniforms. We wanted something to remind us of where we had been, and when we got home we wanted to be able to pull those buttons out of our pockets and say to our families, "See, this is what I have been doing for the last five years."*

And so the Reverend Hardin thought, along with thousands of others, that he was through with the fear and the violence, only to find it had followed the returning men back to Texas, along with the dust and the blood and the proud death.

We walked away from it once, he thought. *Maybe we can again. Maybe I can.*

With that hope in mind, and a half dozen moves later, the Reverend Hardin came to Comanche County and there he bought a farm.

After a while, it began to look as if he had indeed been able to walk off and leave his troubles behind—until now. Now, he stood beside the wagon, thinking, So what is this I see? What shape is that and what horse? What gun and sword and rope? What reason and what purpose?

Once again he saw the hooded figures shrouded in dust and hate and vengeance, riding the fiery black steeds across the scar-streaked face of night, their arms flailing through the dark air, their swords flashing in the moonlight, their nooses at the ready. He heard once more, in the terrible silence, the long forgotten cries, the blood-welling screams of terror and death, and in his heart he felt the clammy grip of the dread unknown.

Still the figure came on, its arms gesturing wildly, its mouth opening and closing on air, with all the motions of speech and shouting but with none of the substance and sound—and beneath it the horse all lathered and fatigued, running on spirit rather than energy or reserve, with its matched, furious hooves shooting soft bullets of dew-damp sand smartly into the air behind it as it came.

By now the rider had cleared the backdrop of the woods, and his own forked nature and the distinctly different one of the quadruped upon which he rode were easily apparent. He was too close anymore to be dismissed as imagination. Even his efforts at shouting were more than just motions now, and what sounded like words were beginning to leave the hinged, flapping mouth to cross the distance as loud and sharp as pistol shots, but still without sense or coherence.

In the time that was left to him, the Reverend Hardin lifted his eyes ever so slightly to regard the smoke that lay thick like fog above and beyond the woods and also above the town. The slight wind was slowly eating it away, beginning along the edges, so that it looked like a blanket beginning to unravel.

So it was the smoke after all, the Reverend Hardin thought, *and that's what he has come to tell me about. I should have been smart enough to unhitch the mules when I first saw it. I should not have tried to deny it. I would have saved a lot of time. What good is your experience if you don't use it? Ten years ago, I would have been a dozen miles away by now. Even a year ago I would have been inside a house with the doors and windows barred and my family on the floor and some kind of gun sitting beside every available window.*

It's just like I don't have to wait for him to get here to know why he is coming and what those pistol-like shouts are all about. I can even tell him while he is waiting to catch his breath and thus save him the trouble, though I will have to ask, "Who was it this time?" or maybe "How many was it this time?" I may also need to ask, "Is it my gun I need to bring or my shovel?"

So why am I standing here? Why don't I just go on and get started?

Julie Ola Faye

When I was fourteen, dere was no glass in de windows, jest boards dat you hang cross to make a latch.

"Leave dat latch down tonight, Honey, and put dat rock neath de window," Ole Jesus say.

I hear de glass breakin somewhere all afternoon jest like I seen him step cool and secret thru de boardless window, comin wid de secret sin and de dark love. In de mornin I git up fore my daddy and go out in de yard and take de rock away.

I was sixteen and never heard bout no Texas or no Hardin or no ole hell fire Jesus weepin oh glory preacher called John Wesley. Not till Mama take me west.

When I was fifteen, my masta take me outa de field and bring me to work in de big house. My mama say to me when I git home, "Here, takes dese ribbons and wraps em round yo breasts so dey wont git down in de bowl when you shellin peas."

"Ah, Mama, dont make fun of me."

"One silver and de other gold. One for yo left breast and one for yo right. Which one does he hold? Which side does he lie on? Put de gold one dere."

"Ah, Mama, dont make fun of me."

"Oh Sweet Jesus! Laud! Laud!" she pray. "Forgive me dis daughter. Forgive us both. You and me has sholy tried to raise us a good child."

I sits in de dark when hit rain and try to hate myself. I

sits in de dark now when hit rain, waitin for de sound of dat glass breakin somewhere. Sometime in de early mornin rain I gits so sad. I miss dat boy off dere in prison and I is fraid for de one dat is burnin down somebodys town. Dat smoke. How tall hit is and hit comin to us thru de woods. I know hit is.

My first masta say to me, "Child, it's too hot for you out here in the field."

And my tits already pushin out at him even den.

"What did you spect?" Mama say.

But pushin out even den till I felt dere is no dress to hold em in. He was lookin at em right thru de dress and dey pushin out at him, trying to reach dem hands. Cause in de night my daddys cousin come in thru de window. He named Jesus by his mother.

"Dont you make a sound," he say. "Here, let me show you what hands is for."

And me jest fourteen. Hit was like nothin I ever felt. Jest like dey was made for hands and other things made for other things.

"If you holler, I kill you," he say.

Den he finish, and I git up and go outside and move de rock from de window.

Den Mama find out.

"Hits dat bad blood in you, child," she say. "We better not let yo daddy find out. He kill Jesus and den he kill you."

"Why don't you come on up to the big house," my first masta say.

Sometime I dream I saddle dis ole white dog and ride off to meet Jesus in de sky, followin my mama on up to heaven.

"I prayin for you, child," she say, fore her eyes wink out. "My sweet little nigger whore."

De death come in and sit on de lids one at a time like two little devils. Cause at first she refused to go. She didnt want to die.

Jest fore Mama die, she paint a picture of dis ole white dog fightin a bear. She draw it wid a pencil so I could not tell it was not him and den color hit wid cake colors. Bear was jest a big pup den.

Dat smoke! Hit must be a mile tall, and John Wesley burnin down de whole town so dey come and hang ever Hardin west of de river. Even dis ole nigger whore who never had no sense to leave when she see de smoke. If hit wasnt for dat ole crippled hog. If I didnt have to kill hit and tug hit up to de pot one leg at a time and den de head and den de rump.

"Come on up to the big house, you dark honey."

Hit must be a mile tall by now standin up dere like a big black nigger man tryin to git a look at dese breasts.

What he mean was, *"Come on up to de big house you sweet thing you so I can git my hands on dem tits."*

Mama say, "Maybe you wont have to work in de field no more after dis."

"It's too hot out here in the field for a young girl like you," he say.

"You dark Honey you," what he mean.

Somebody say to us, "This dog is a fine dog."

Hit was ole Isham Hicks dat de Indians cut his hair for him. He say, "This here ain't no ordinary dog. This here is a bear hound. A pyrenees bear hound." So mama paint him fightin a bear and jest fore she die she asks for de picture.

"Bring my paintin in here so I can set eyes on hit fore I go. See how fierce and proud dat ole dog is?"

"Yes, Mama," I says.

"See how strong and unafraid and hateful of bears dat ole dog is?"

"Yes, Mama," I say

"I is jest dat way wid dis death. I hate hit so much jest like dat dog hate bears. I gonna fight hit and fight hit as long as I can."

Den one night she die. Death come in thru de window and set on her eyes like two little devils. Now dat ole dog hangs on de wall still fightin wid dat bear and when he kill hit one day, he step out of de picture and I put a saddle on him and we rides off to find if Jesus has compassion for nigger whores dat only left de boards off de window and set up a rock for a step.

Hit be dark fore dey come in from celebratin John Wesley's birthday. I has to haul dat ole hog and pull on hit and hit too big for no man much less a nigger woman wid no help but dis boy and dat ole white dog. Maybe we use one of dem asleep mules to haul hit up on a limb and cut hits throat so hit will bleed all dat hot sticky blood.

"Hits too late to kill hit," I says to Masta Johnny. "Hit wont keep. Hit will ruin, broke leg or no broke leg."

"You are too young at fifteen to work in the field," my first masta say. What he mean was, *"Come on up to de house, you dark little Honey."*

Dat smokes so tall and so black I oughta be runnin. Whatever hit mean hit dont mean no good to me or to no other nigger. I oughta go wherever ole devil nigger whores go when dere aint no place else dey can go. I aint never been no good for nothin.

When I was sixteen, I jest lay dere listenin to what dat ole preacher have to say, lettin his words come down on me and roll on off carryin wid em my sin and his sin, feelin his hands and mouth all over me, sayin de words of de Laud dat was cleansin me out and scrubbin me clean and pure wid de brush of his holy word. Jest layin dere in de dark wid his hands and mouth all over me, sayin "Laud how we hate dis daughter of Lilith for your sake, Laud. How we need to drive de soft long haired Lilith devil out of dis child" and him spillin all over me like soured syrup.

Den I was fifteen, draggin dat eight foot sack like a dead turtle tryin to get three hundred pounds fore dark so I could ride up on top of all dat soft cotton to de gin. Den he come to de field and git me.

"You are so soft and round and you just fifteen, you little Honey you."

Dis time de mattress had cotton in hit stead of corn shucks and dat was when I know dese tits like white mens hands as good as black mens hands.

Dat smoke is comin. I know hit is. I can hear de glass

breakin and you oughta be runnin, you ole nigger whore. Cept first I got to git dat pot boilin and den git dat gun from behind de door. Cept I dont aim to use hit. Sticks better. My ole daddy say he could hit so dey jest tremble once fore dey die. Dat was de way I learn. But gun or stick dont make no difference. Hit ruin fore we can eat hit no how.

When Eldora was sold, my daddys cousin Jesus didnt have no girl to marry, but he was sho pretty. All creamy white.

"Now listen," he say. "A man gets all kind of devilment in him when he aint got no woman, and you is sho nice. I aint ask your daddy yet, but I aim to take good care of you. I will build you a porch on de front of my house dat you can sit under. I aint gonna go workin you to death in de field either, a girl as pretty as yourself. But I aint said nothing to your daddy yet and dont you tell him."

Dat night he come to my bed thru de window where I left de boards off. Like he say.

"Dont you holler," he say, and his hands was workin, showin me what hands was for.

Den I was fifteen, draggin dat eight foot sack like a dead turtle, and I never heard of no John Wesley Hardin dat killed folks cause dey was usin de same road like he was. I didnt know what glass was. If hit was jest me and dis ole white dog I would leave, but I is a nigger and I caint leave. A niggers life is all trouble and work. First dere is cotton and when hits planted and all laid by and picked and de corn all hauled and scooped into de bin by hand, den you can git ready for de spring so you can walk behind de plow from sun to sun.

Dats when I know I is lucky to be born a nigger. Like dat ole preacher say, wid dat bad blood de way hit was. Else I would be on my back lookin up at some ceilin all my life. Oh Sweet Jesus, I is a awful ole whore. Even at forty I is still havin to fight bein a whore. If he was jest not a preacher wid dat Bible strapped round his middle, den I could say to him— Den I could shed dese ole heavy sins and kneel down fore him and confess.

"Laud, Laud," Id say, *"dese four hands has sinned."*

And hit was four men by 1869. Four and him jest a boy yet.

"You are the only nigger I have ever loved, Mama Julie Ola Faye," he say to me. "You are like my own mother to me. If I didn't have a mother, you would be my mother."

Him fightin me at de tits till dey was so sore dat later I would say to my man, "Be careful, Honey, dat hurts some where dat baby been. Dat hurts."

Den he growed and say to me, *"Mama Julie Ola Faye, when I die time will stop for five minutes. People will cry out in the streets 'John Wesley Hardin is dead!' and take their watches from their pockets and note the time and then smash them, saying, 'The old time is done! Johnny Boy is dead!'"*

And Jesus comin in thru de glassless window in de night sayin, *"I wants to commit sin. I wants to commit adultery. I desire fornication. To lick and suck and feel all things evil and sinful and shameful and lustful wid you, you sweet Julie Ola Faye child. I wants to wallow on you. I wants to die de sweet death on you, you little honey. I wants to die de sweet death and den leave on Angels wings thru de boardless window."*

I been havin dat dream all my life. Oh come to me, Sweet Jesus. Sweet J. W. Jesus.

I been hearin dat glass breakin all afternoon. Dat smoke is comin, and I oughta go hide in de church. Cept dere aint no church for niggers in Texas. Mama hear bout one once but hits too far. No Jesus for niggers here neither. But when I was sixteen, Mama say to dat preacher, "Dis here girl got de bad blood. Pray for her. Preach to her."

Dat preacher say, "Honey, lets us talk bout yo bad blood."

Dats when I knowed dat preachers had hands jest like other men, but first he prayed.

"Oh Laud," he say, "let dis here girl git clean of her bad blood. Use me, Laud. Let dis here colored gal git clean. Use me as yo instrument, Laud. Let me be de instrument to bring yo love and forgiveness to dis here stray lamb. Like lye soap on a washday, Laud, clean her in and clean her out till she shine. Let me be dat instrument, like Paul changed on de Demascus road. Let her be lifted up. Yes, Jesus!"

And den he say, "Oh, thank you, Sweet Jesus. Yes, Laud. Oh, thank you, Sweet Jesus."

Next he say, "Now pray child. Be thankful unto de Laud, for he has heard your plea and he has forgiven you. He tell me to be de instrument of his power. Let you and me go up to de house and talk some more bout dat bad blood."

Dats when I knowed no ole preacher caint save me. I knowed Jesus and de Bible caint save me, neither. Hit didnt save my boy when he got dat whiskey and hit didnt save dem four men J.W. Jesus shot.

My mama say to me, "I has six chillun. One was kicked by a mule in de head and one died of de fever. One I roll on in de night and smother in de bed. Ole Masta shot one cause he stealin food and one become a Baptist peacher and run off to Memphis. Den I got one whore name Julie Ola Faye. Aint I lucky I has so many fine chillum! Laud, Laud! Aint de Laud takin good care of dis ole nigger woman!"

Dat smokes comin. Somethins comin. I caint see hit yet. I caint hear hit yet but hits comin. Oh, Laud, help dis ole nigger whore wid de bad blood. Masta Johnny, hits comin. I wish I was where ole niggers go when dey aint burned down no town. Oh, hide me lost sweet Mama.

"Lilith de first woman de Laud made," de preacher say, "but she wouldn't love her husband. She was an adulterous whore."

"Wid who?" I say.

"Jest a whore," he say, "and de Laud turn her out of de Garden of Eden and made Eve in her place and now she is in de wind at night and in de rain when hit storms, wailin in her misery, settin in trees and on de tops of mountains and poured into de white sand, her long hair flamin down over de earth bringin pain and trouble and sorrow."

"Amen! Go on, Preacher! Preach hit!"

But Adam didnt have no two wives. It say right dere in de Bible he had one wife.

Oh, hide me, lost sweet Mama, de mother of all ole nigger whores, hidin in de wind, lurkin in de rain at night, callin out de names of her lost daughters. Sometime I think de rain is de sweetest sound I ever heard.

If me and dis boy and dat ole white dog was jest up dere jerkin on dat rope right now, gittin ready to cut hits throat so hit would bleed. If we jest was, cause him sittin up dere on dat wagon readin dat Bible aint gonna help nobody jest like hit aint gonna stop nothin from comin out of dem woods cause hits comin no way.

"Isn't this much better up here in the big house than out there in that old hot field? Why don't you just lie back here on this bed, Honey, and let me get you something cool to drink."

Jesus is comin' thru de window at night sayin *"I wants to commit—."* Oh laudy and me gittin ready to cut hits throat so hit can bleed and wash me clean.

Dat preacher say when I sixteen, "Now, Honey, let me put down dis Bible so we can see how bad yo blood is. Here, let me feel how bad yo blood is."

Aint no ole Bible gonna help nothin from comin out of dem woods bringin what hits bringin. Hit caint help no ole nigger whore stop hit neither, not even to help dem she love. Oh, I can hear de glass breakin somewhere.

"Masta Johnny!"

Jim Stephens

After the death of Turner Evans, although separated by six years from the later event, it was but a short step to Wes's killing of a Negro named Mage. As one killing preceded the other in time, just as surely one indirectly caused the other—or rather made it possible. Following Mage, the next several years saw a long string of trouble beginning with the knifing of Charley Sloter in '67 and ending in the town of Comanche in '74, when Wes and I would finally go our different ways.

The years I had with Wes were good years, though looking back on them now from the vantage point of the dawn of a new century it is hard to understand why I would say that. Sometimes I have trouble remembering myself. But I keep coming back to the fact that those years just after the war were violent times, as violent as any this country has seen. It must also be remembered that people did not always have the liberty of choosing to avoid that violence. Though some did choose it as a way of life, others were thrust into the middle of it without choice. Once caught in this spinning web, it was all but impossible to break free. That I was able to do it and Wes was not I cannot fully explain. I don't understand it myself. I do believe, however, that violence has a life of its own. Though we may know full well its drastic consequences and would avoid it if at all possible, once its shadow settles in on us it changes life as we know it—as we would have chosen to live it.

On the fateful day in question, Wes and I decided to take
a short trip down to his Uncle Barnett Hardin's place in Polk
County. The farm lay about four miles north of Livingstone,
and Wes was by then fifteen years old. It was fall, and Barnett
and his boys were working cane. As Wes's father wanted a
batch of syrup in store for the winter, we set out with no
thought but to make the trip down, procure the syrup, and
return the next day. About three miles before reaching Uncle
Barnett's farm, we came upon a gang of men and boys gathered
in a clearing, engaged in a friendly wrestling match. One of
the boys was a cousin of Wes's by the name of Barnett Jones.
Of course, Wes wanted to try his hand, and he and his cousin
were soon matched against a large powerful Negro named
Mage. It should have been no match at all, but by some
combination of luck and skill the two boys managed to throw
the Negro to the ground. The fall surprised the boys as much
as it did the Negro, who insisted on being given another
chance. The second match ended as the first, with the Negro
on the ground, only this time without intending to do so Wes
scratched Mage on his face.

When the Negro got up, he was mad. He said he could
whip Wes and would do it right then. Although the Negro was
twice his size, Wes was just fool enough to fight. Before the
situation could get any worse, some of the men held Mage
back and sent us boys on to Uncle Barnett's house. This move
made the Negro madder than ever, if that was possible. He
yelled out at us, saying he would kill Wes if he ever saw him
again, or die trying. He said no white boy could draw his blood
and live and that a bird never flew too high not to come to the
ground.

By next morning Wes and I had put the matter of Mage
behind us and were concerned only with transporting the
syrup back to Wes's family. At the last moment we decided to
go a bit out of the way in order to visit Captain Sam Rowes,
an old friend of the Hardin family. We were about six miles
from the captain's place when we came upon the Negro Mage
walking along the same road we were following through the

woods. He recognized us at once and began to curse and abuse Wes, calling him a coward for not staying around to fight the day before. Wes explained it had only been a friendly match and that he had not intended to hurt Mage, but the Negro would have none of it. He was easily as belligerent as the day before and arrogant and boastful in the way only a Reconstruction Negro could be who had got it into his head that a war had been fought for his benefit and that its outcome gave him the right to push around every white son of a bitch who got in his way.

Finally, Wes saw that talking wasn't going to work, so we turned off the road and tried to go another direction, thinking that even though our horses were loaded down with gallon syrup jugs in addition to carrying riders, we could easily outrun Mage. "If I can but get hold of you, I will kill you and throw you in that creek," Mage yelled after us. At this we urged our horses into a trot, but the Negro on seeing what we had in mind began to run, cutting across through the woods and coming out in front of us again.

"And don't think to outrun me!" he yelled when he had gained the advantage again. "Not on that horse you won't!"

Wes was riding an old paint horse at the time, a poor one, and he knew Mage was right. But by now Mage had hold of the bridle and was hitting at Wes with a big stick he had picked up in the woods. The first time he hit Wes, Wes pulled out a Colt .44 six shooter he had won in a poker game a week or so before and shot it off in the air above the Negro's head. This did not stop Mage, and the next time he hit Wes across the shoulder and along one side, almost knocking him off his horse. Wes shot Mage then, with the bullet breaking his hold on the bridle but not knocking him down. He caught the bridle once more and drew back his stick to hit again, and Wes shot him loose a second time. To put Mage on the ground to stay, Wes had to shoot him still a third time. Even then the Negro was cussing at him and trying to raise himself up.

While I stayed with Mage, Wes rode to get Uncle Clabe Houlshousen. Despite our efforts to save him, Mage died shortly after Uncle Clabe's arrival. Uncle Clabe then gave Wes a $20 dollar gold piece and advised us to be on our way. He told us to buy enough supplies for a month and then go someplace and hide out. When we got home and told Wes's father what had happened, he became afraid for us and like Uncle Clabe told us to go into hiding until there was a chance for a fair trial. At that time the state and the courts were being run by carpetbaggers and bureau agents who were enemies of the South and who administered a code of justice pretty much to suit themselves. To be tried during that reconstruction period for the killing of a Negro meant almost certain death, no matter what the circumstances. Wes's father was afraid to chance it. Of course, he was right, though at the time I had no notion of the implications involved in what we were about to do. Neither did Wes I think. We were caught up in the excitement of hiding out and being on our own. All in all, the incident was a good example, as I have said, of violence which you would avoid if you could, but which once thrust upon you, you cannot refuse to deal with.

Wes and I left immediately and went to Navarro County where we hid out in some woods along a creek, doing a little hunting and trying to round up a few wild cattle. It was a peaceful enough place for a while. We worked hard during the day and ate a good full meal around the fire at night and then went off to sleep looking up at the stars, trying to see what kinds of patterns were there.

Then someone turned us in. One day we were riding down the bed of the creek when we met up with three United States soldiers who demanded our surrender. In the battle that followed, both Wes and I shot a half dozen times each. When it was over, the three soldiers lay dead along the banks of the creek, two of them white and one colored. I do not know if I killed one alone but am certain my bullets were in all three before we had finished. We had no choice. They would have killed us for certain had we given over our guns. That realization made it easy to kill them. Even Wes admitted he felt no guilt as he had with Mage.

The soldiers had ridden up on us out of nowhere and demanded our six shooters and Wes's shotgun.

"We are United States soldiers who have been sent out to find you and bring you in for trial for killing the Negro Mage," one of them announced. "Will you give us your guns or will we be forced to take them? Come, give us your answer!"

"I can't speak for my friend there, but here is my answer!" Wes said.

With that, Wes spurred his horse into their middle so they couldn't shoot at him without fear of hitting each other. I heard Wes's shotgun explode twice and then his Colt .44. In a minute or less it was over. We buried the bodies of the soldiers in the bed of the creek and turned their horses over to friends of ours and so everything was kept quiet.

Once again, it had not been difficult to kill the soldiers. Few Texans had any love for the Reconstruction government and no more for the men who enforced its policies. I saw Wes and myself as heroes. Despite our attempts to keep the matter under cover, however, news got out that John Wesley Hardin, a fifteen-year-old boy, had already killed four times. Men all over the counties were beginning to talk about him, a few to blame him as an outlaw and a ruthless killer who should be hanged, but most to praise him as defender and preserver of the same Texas spirit which had brought in the Republic some years before.

And that's how the legend of John Wesley Hardin got started. Once it did, there seemed no end to it. Late in 1869, Wes killed a fifth man over a poker game down in Hill County and before we could get out of there he had to kill a sixth man, a circus hand near a place called Horn Hill. It was cold that night, and Wes and I along with several other men were standing close about the fire, trying to stay warm. While reaching to pour himself some coffee, Wes accidently bumped the hand of this circus fellow, causing him to drop his pipe into the fire. For that, the man knocked Wes down, meaning to shoot him, but Wes drew his .44 and shot the man in the head before he could get his gun free.

After that, Wes and I left for Brenham, but on the way Wes got involved with a woman and was accosted that same night by her sweetheart. The man drew down on Wes and demanded his money, thinking to kill Wes as soon as he got it. Somehow Wes got the drop on him and killed him where he stood. That made seven men by the end of 1869. Following that incident, I no longer tried to keep a count. I let popular gossip do it for me, and naturally Wes kept a kind of record cut into the willow tally stick he carried in his pocket, but it wasn't accurate. He forgot from one town to the next. He got the men he killed mixed up with the men he had only shot, and of course, we never knew if some of the men died eventually or went on to recover. We did not stay to make inquiries.

In January of 1870 Wes and I reached Brenham and went on directly to the farm of Uncle Bob Hardin where we stayed through the spring. We helped with the work of putting in the spring crops and made frequent trips into Brenham to drink and gamble. It was in Brenham that Wes picked up the name "Young Seven-Up," a tribute to his skill in that game of chance. Our visits there also brought us into contact with a number of notorious men, one of whom was Phil Coe, destined to be killed in Abilene, Kansas, by Wild Bill some years later.

One Saturday Wes and I made a side trip to Evergreen, a well known race town filled with hard characters about forty miles from Brenham. It was there we met another notorious bad man, Bill Longley. This is how it came about.

Wes was playing "seven-up" with Ben Hines and had won upwards of $20 dollars from him. When Wes decided to quit playing and go get something to eat, Hines got mad. He had the reputation of being one of the most dangerous men in the country, a character who would not be trifled with.

"Why, you little S.O.B.!" Hines said to Wes. "If you were not a boy, I would beat you to death!"

"I stand in man's shoes!" Wes replied. "Don't let my youth spoil a good intention."

"You damned little impudent scoundrel! I'll beat hell out

of you!"

At that, Hines made a grab for Wes, only to find the barrel of Wes's .44 sticking in his chest. Other men had come up by now, and a couple tried to get in behind Wes.

"The first man who makes a move or draws a gun I will kill him!" Wes yelled.

After that, the men backed off, and Hines apologized for his outburst. He could do little else with Wes's pistol stuck in his chest that way.

"Young man, I was wrong. I beg your pardon. You are a giant with a youth's face. Even if you are a boy I bow to you, and here is my hand in good faith."

"I cannot take your hand," Wes told him, "but I accept your apology in good faith."

"Then I will be your friend," Hines replied. "Don't be uneasy while you are here. Bill Longley will be at the races tomorrow, so stop over and we will have a good time."

Wes and I went on to eat our dinner and then spent most of the afternoon looking over some of the horses which would be running in the race next day. Toward evening, we were approached by a shady-looking, rude-mannered man who identified himself as Bill Longley.

"My name is Bill Longley," he said to Wes. "I believe you are a spy for McAnally. If you don't watch out, you will be shot all to pieces before you know it."

I think Longley was testing Wes as much as he was making an accusation, but he got more than he bargained for.

"You believe a damned lie!" Wes told him. "All I ask is that those who are going to do the shooting will get in front of me. All I ask is a fair fight, and if your name is Bill Longley I want you to understand that you can't bulldoze or scare me!"

Longley replied, "I see I have made a mistake. Are you here to see the races?"

"Not particularly."

Following this encounter, Longley invited Wes and me to participate in a poker game he had been headed for when he struck us. Both Longley and Wes got in, and when it came

Wes's turn to deal, he found himself with three jacks and so raised $5. All the players stayed in, and on the draw Longley took three cards and the other two players two each. Wes also drew two and got the other jack. As it turned out, Longley filled on aces, one of the other players had a flush, and the third filled on queens. A couple of bets were made, first $5 better and then $10 better. With each man confident in his hand, the ante was up considerable when it came Wes's turn to bet. After thinking it over, Wes said, "You can't run me out on my own deal, so I go $10 better."

"Well, stranger, you have your foot in it now," Longley said. "I go you $50 better."

Wes studied for some time, as if he couldn't decide what to do.

Longley became impatient and urged Wes to bet or fold.

"Well, stranger," he said. "It's up to you. What do you do?"

"What are you betting, 'wind or money'?" Wes asked.

"Money!" Longely replied.

"Put it up."

Longley took four $20 gold pieces out of one pocket and put them down and then a $5 gold piece out of another pocket.

"All right," Wes said. "Here is your $50 and I go you $250 better."

Longley replied, "I go you. I call you."

"Then put up your money."

"Will my word not do?" Longley asked.

"Not here."

Out of a third pocket, Longley pulled eleven $20 gold pieces.

"I call you for $220," he said.

"I reckon you have me beat," Wes said, pushing his chair back and appearing to fold his hand.

"I reckon so. I have got an ace full."

Longley thought he had Wes then, but I had watched Wes play long enough that I knew better. He would never have gone this far if he wasn't sure of what he had.

"Hold on, I have two pair," he said.

"They are not worth a damn!" Longley said, still certain of his victory.

Then Wes let the hammer down.

"I reckon two pair of jacks are good," he said. By the time we left town that evening, Wes was ahead by $300.

In January 1871 Wes killed a man named Jim Smolly near Waco. In attempting to get away, we were captured near Belton by three men calling themselves state police. We managed to get hold of a couple of pistols that night while they slept and killed all three of them where they lay. Other scuffles followed, and by the spring of 1871 we were up along the South Canadian near Red River Station working cattle. Not long after we arrived, Wes shot an Indian who was following us while we worked. Later on, he shot another one he caught stealing a couple of the cattle we were driving north to Kansas.

On the way up the trail to Abilene, we ran into trouble with some Mexican drovers. Before that was settled, we had killed six of them, with Wes claiming five of them as his own, though in reality he didn't number Mexicans among the men he had killed. I don't know if other people felt the same way or not. Memory of the Alamo was still strong in Texas and shooting a Mexican was like shooting a skunk. You were expected to do it, and no one blamed you if you did. But counting the Mexicans or not made little difference. By that time neither of us had an accurate notion how many men Wes had killed. It didn't seem to make a difference any more. There toward the end, when both the rumors and the notches on Wes's tally stick were nearing forty, Wes said that number sounded about right, if we didn't include the Mexicans and Indians and also left off those who had managed to live more than twenty-four hours after they were shot.

During those heady days, it seemed we could do anything we wanted and get away with it. In Abilene the Marshall was Wild Bill, the famous killer. By this time, Wes had a considerable reputation of his own, and while we were there Wes backed Wild Bill down a couple of times and lived to tell about it. He had been watching for Wild Bill anyway because he suspected Bill of wanting to kill him simply to add to his own reputation. Wes had reached the point where he wouldn't tolerate any kind of pushing, though I will admit that when we left Abilene the last time we left in the middle of the night, running for our lives.

As the months went by, we moved from one town to another in northeast and north central Texas, never staying in one place for long, and soon the notches on the tally stick went all the way down one side and almost all the way back up the other. In 1874, we found ourselves drifting back toward Comanche County where I was born. The entire Hardin family had moved out there by then, onto a small farm about four miles west of town. There Wes's father, J. G. Hardin, did a little farming and some preaching, while Wes's brother Joe practiced law in the town of Comanche itself.

Wes had married Jane by now, though he had not been able to spend much time with her. That was one reason we were going home. Wes was twenty years old at the time, and I was seventeen, almost eighteen. It had been years since I had been to Comanche and seen my brother and sisters. Needless to say, I was also looking forward to seeing the Hardin clan, whom I looked upon as my second family. I especially wanted to see Julie Ola Faye. I hoped it would rain while we were there and I could slip off down to her cabin again and listen to the rain hitting against the tin on the roof. I hoped, like all the times before, that she would talk to me about how it had been when she was a young girl—how her mother had all those children and the sad ways some of them had died; how she used to let her cousin Jesus into her bed at night through the window that didn't have any glass in it and each morning go out and take the rock from under the window so her daddy wouldn't know; and how later a preacher that her mother took her to claimed he was saving her soul by crawling into bed with her. They were always the same tales, but I never got tired of hearing them. Julie had a past deep and dark, filled with poverty and misery and sadness and shame, but she loved to talk about it. She was a fine Negro woman, a striking and pretty woman, even if she was old enough to be my mother.

Anonymous

When he could watch the rider no longer, his nerve failing, the Reverend Hardin dropped his eyes and swung around to the Negro woman where she stood at the edge of the field. She had not moved, her stance and position like his own, unchanged from when she first spoke and with the shape of the word *Masta* still formed on her lips as though she thought she might have to repeat it. She stood leaning on the hoe, supported by it somewhat with the end of the handle resting between her great breasts and against her chest like a third leg grown just for that moment. On her left stood the thin brown child and on her right, sitting on wide splayed haunches, the huge white bear dog, all watching the man and the horse as they crossed the remaining distance between the woods and the waiting wagon.

For the briefest of moments it looked as though the Reverend Hardin intended finally to move, to leave his position by the wagon and go to the woman. He saw her feet spread ever so slightly, to support her thighs and belly and her great breasts, along with the help of the hoe, and what he saw was strangely but strongly comforting. Leaning a little forward, she had positioned her body as though she intended never to yield her ground, even so much as an inch, seeming for all the world to be pointing herself at the man on the horse like a cannon arched and ready to shoot off.

This is how the Reverend Hardin saw her anyway, as a cannon, and a quick thought ran through his mind, only it was not thought. It was deeper than thought, and older, perhaps even unthinkable after all, and yet if he could have expressed it, it would have been, *Out of something like that I came, not so plentiful, not so opulent, but out of something like that we all came. Oh great sweet Mother, take me back and enfold me now in love and protection.*

The Reverend saw also the Negro's heavy, full breasts, sagged down and out against the thin cotton dress. He saw her belly round and smooth and her chocolate marble thighs where her dress had been hiked up for cooling, and he felt as the prophets of old upon consideration of end time—*There is where I must go. Oh, sweet valleys and hills and mountains, hide me. Take me into yourself and wrap yourself around me and hide me that I may be warm and safe from the oncoming apocalyptic conflagration. Oh, hide me and love me and keep me safe and warm, great sweet Mother.*

And yet, seeing the woman that way, feeling that about her, the Reverend Hardin still would not move, or could not. Then the phantom, floating horse and its rider were upon him. In a furious blinding instant as though some giant unseen hand had plucked them up, lifted them bodily, and moved them suddenly the last quarter of a mile and set them down again in front of the Reverend Hardin, they were now trying both to stop and yet still to run, as if neither horse nor man could decide what to do. It ended finally in a flurry of flashing hooves and splayed legs with the man's arms jerking and restraining, yet still gesturing wildly.

Out of that confusion the first sounds began to emerge that were neither pounding nor creaking nor snorting nor cussing, sounds broken and mostly incoherent.

"—that fire—that smoke that you see there—my god man, aren't you—haven't you guessed yet? That smoke that you see rising up out of the center of town—well, I guess I don't have to tell you, of all people!"

Those few halting, breathless words had slipped out amid the furious snorting and cartwheelings of the horse who by now had turned itself around where it stood, and did it with all four feet up in the air like a circus animal, managing to use its last twisting forward motion to launch itself into some kind of terrific backward spin so that when it came down again, feet churning, its head was pointed back in the direction it had come. Meanwhile, the man, still in the saddle, with head turned now back over his shoulder, was trying once more to say what he had come to say before the horse could carry him off again.

"—now come on, Man! Hurry! Hurry! It may even be too late to hurry, but come on!"

Before the rider the black-clothed figure of the Reverend Hardin stood unmoved, appearing no longer to listen, if he had ever listened at all. Nothing that had been said or even the circus horse switching ends six inches in front of his face had caused him even to blink.

Now, with the rider rapidly receding and halfway to the wood again, the Reverend turned and calmly begin to take the white mule out of its harness, doing it rapidly yet without apparent haste so that he was nearly finished by the time the last panic screamed words *"Hurry now, man"* leaked out of the cloud of dust and sweat and confused motion that was the disappearing rider and his horse.

Only then did the Reverend Hardin speak.

"Wait!" he cried out.

With that, the rider stopped, as unmoving now in silhouette as before he had been furious and frenzied—stopped and rode back to the Reverend Hardin and got down off the horse so that for the first time the two men could actually look one another in the eye.

"To hell with the smoke and fire!" the Reverend said. "Just tell me about Wes and Joe!"

And the one standing by the horse replied, "I don't know that! Would I be out here now if I knew that! Would I have ridden like hell four miles on the back of one of these crazy coyotes of Wes's if I had known that?"

But he said it too loud for men standing within a foot of one another, too hurried also as if he were still astride the raging horse, still swirling in confusion. What is more, he had a sharpness to his voice as if he might really like to say, "Do you actually believe there is anything, even money, that could have persuaded me to ride out here on one of these circus freaks? You have seen these Comanche County monkeys before. Even you know what they're like, and you have just seen this one turn completely around in less space than a mosquito would need—even a whole lot of money, since what good is money if you are too dead to spend it? Maybe I would stand beside a race track with a fence between me and them and spend money betting on which one of them was crazier than another one of them and so faster and more likely to win, but I'll be damned if I'd crawl on one just to come tell you what has already happened that you are too late to do anything about anyway. Or even to come tell you what you already know. Hell, I have a horse of my own, a damn good horse, else I would not own it. But what Wes needed most and what he had least of when I last saw him is what you are now wasting as if you had all of it in the world. I'm talking about time. So I said, 'Hell, saddle me up one of them crazy coyotes and whisper in his ear it's just one more race and that you've got money put down on him and then get out of the way. I'll try to keep him guided in the right direction!' And all that because I thought the few minutes I might save would be at least as important to you whose son he is as they were to me who am nothing but his friend. So damn your indifference, anyway! Damn your questions, too!"

The man could also see himself catching the Reverend up bodily and throwing him across the front of the horse and then mounting himself, saying as they began to run once more toward town, "At least can't nobody say I didn't do what I came out here to do just like they won't be able to say you weren't there to watch it all take place. Maybe I can't make you act like a father should. Maybe I won't even try anymore. But if we hurry maybe we can get there in time to see him kicking a little on the end of that rope."

Beyond that the man saw himself rushing back into town

and across the square and there, beneath the hanging tree, flinging the Reverend Hardin off onto the ground below the dangling feet of his son, saying, "Here is your father. I have brought him the way you asked me to do."

"But where—what?" the Reverend Hardin asked.

"You mean I have to tell you that, too? You mean you haven't guessed yet? It's the—"

"—blacksmith shop there on the southwest corner across from the bank?"

"Yes!"

"Of course, what else could it be? Was there ever any doubt? Okay, maybe I am a little slow, but just tell me this— no, wait! I'm not asking about the other again. I realize you don't know what else or as you said you would still be on your way out here since there wouldn't be any reason left to hurry. But at least tell me this—Martin Flemming's old Black Jack Oak where he hid out from the Indians when he was a boy, had they—did they have any—as you were leaving did you take time to see if they—"

"Yes, Man! That's what I have been trying to tell you. Haven't you heard anything I've said? Why do you think we need to hurry?"

And once again the man could see himself lifting the Reverend bodily and hauling him into town and there tossing him on the ground like a sack of oats and watching him bounce a little on the hard tamped clay beneath the gallows tree. Actually enjoying it too. But then he calmed himself.

"Yes, four ropes that I could see, and what is more—"

But by now, the Reverend Hardin was no longer listening. He had the mule loose and was on a dead run along the side of the wagon, doing a little thinking of his own for the first time since he'd seen the rider clear the woods. Then he too had a vision, of sorts. He saw himself riding into town, leading an army, yelling out to people he passed along the road, "I am J. G. Hardin, and if you know what's good for you, you will stay out of my way and you will for damn sure not try to stop me!"

But it wasn't an ordinary army he led, not one of mere men, but an army of angels, archangels arrayed in gleaming battle dress, carrying in their uplifted hands great gleaming swords of righteousness and justice and wearing on their holy, shining faces the glory and indignation and wrath of the almighty God.

It was as if the Reverend had done it all before, as if he had been to the same place before on the same mission. That time it had been a hill outside Jerusalem and another time in the temple where he scattered the money changers and once too on the Assyrian Heights when in a matter of minutes he had destroyed by half and singlehandedly the forces of the enemies of Israel. Then again in Egypt with the blood and the fiery hail and the parting waters and before that the great flood.

Now inside his head the Reverend heard the thunder cracking and beneath his feet felt the rolling unsteady earth with all nature trembling and cowed before him, and somewhere in the distance voices lifted on high sang to the accompaniment of harps—"Almighty God, Joshua and Saul and David and Alexander and Caesar and Hannibal and a hundred others—have slain their thousands but Hardin has slain his ten thousands."

Finally, the Reverend saw himself entering the square and taking the still breathing body of his son down off Martin Flemming's old Live Oak cross. He saw himself taking an ax and cutting the oak to the ground and burning it where it fell and behind him the archangels massed more numerous than the stars on a hundred nights, all of them lifted up and beating their luminous wings in unison so that the sound was that of a giant base fiddle or of the voice of God booming out of a thunder cloud, "I am God! I am that I am, and this is my servant, J. G. Hardin, on a mission of divine justice and mercy!"

When the Reverend could stop thinking long enough to get back to what he was doing, he ran around to the back of the wagon, where after a mad fevered rummaging through the junk piled there he pulled out a battered double-barrel shotgun with the barrels sawed off at least a foot. Then he ran back to the mule.

"Just tell me one more thing," he said. "Who was it this time. Was it that—"

"Charley Webb!" the man said. "A deputy sheriff come over from Brown County—in the street beside the saloon— once in the left cheek below the eye and one time each in the stomach and side."

By the time the man finished speaking, the Reverend Hardin had mounted the mule and was kicking it savagely in the flanks.

"Move you white bastard, you! Move!" he yelled, at the same time beating the mule across the rump with the flat of the shotgun barrels until as if launched from a loaded spring the mule leaped a dozen feet forward and was maybe fifteen cotton rows in front of the wagon before either the man or his horse realized what had happened. Then over his shoulder as he urged the mule on, the shotgun swinging wildly in his free hand, the Reverend shouted back to the Negro woman in the field.

"You go on home now, Julie Ola Faye!" he yelled. "You kill that hog like I told you to. And whatever you do, don't come into town! You make damn sure you don't show yourself in town!"

Turning back, the Reverend galloped on toward the rapidly growing woods, his eyes set on the almost hidden opening where the trail emerged, thinking again as he rode, *I should not have named him that. I should never have. What could I have been thinking? A name that has no peace in death could not hope to have more in life. A name that has bloodied half of England and some of Europe too could not but expect to shed a little more in Texas. Even if he aint no preacher. Even if I never intended that he be any kind of preacher. But it doesn't make any difference now. I just never should have. I should have been older, wiser, or maybe I thought older was wiser or that there was some other path to wisdom than misfortune.*

Well, that folly I have certainly paid for! That folly was sure enough damned expensive! I would sure like to have been the party that collected the interest on that loan! They ask what's in a name? Now I can tell them. Once I wouldn't have been able to. A whole lot of damned trouble, for sure!

Behind the Reverend Hardin, the man on the horse had finally recovered himself enough to start forward in pursuit, but race nag or no race nag the four miles out had tired the horse, and almost as soon as it started to run again it slowed. Then the man began to kick it and cuss at it just as the Reverend had done with the mule.

"Come on, you crazy coyote! Run now, you smart bastard, you! I thought you were supposed to be some kind of a race horse! Well, somebody must have made a mistake about that! Now run, goddamn you, run!"

And here the man kicked it hard, savagely in the side and continued to do so until it had begun to lope—not running really, but faster than a trot.

"All right, come on now!" the man yelled, leaning down close over one ear. "Pretend I have just bet one hundred dollars on you and that I am going to shoot you if you lose! So come on now and run! There is something I forgot to tell Preacher Hardin. Something he needs to know!"

And the man urged the horse on, thinking now, Something that might make some little amount of difference even yet— that it was self-defense after a fashion since Webb drew first and shot first and the only crime that has really been committed was the sheriff's since he knew John Wesley was in town but didn't go on to collect all the other guns in town besides John Wesley's, and knives too, while he was at it, since it has been proved that whenever there is a gun or a knife around anywhere sooner or later somebody is going to lay hands on it for the solitary purpose of trying to kill John Wesley. Hell, the sheriff knew that! He knew too that what you can call suicide on one man's part you can call self-defense on another man's part, and suicide is obviously what Charley Webb had in mind. Except the law don't work that way. The law as set down in statutes and books never heard of a John Wesley Hardin. To the law, self-defense is still self-defense. There aint no provision that says a man must be allowed not only the first shot but two more in addition else it is murder to kill him, because the law as it is set down in books never allowed for a John Wesley Hardin. It never knew to. So there is still that chance—if they can get him up to New York or somewhere east where they aint never heard that name apart from its association with religion and there pick an impartial jury, then maybe he has a chance. I forgot to tell Preacher Hardin that. It just might make a difference.

"So run, you lathered bastard, you! You useless excuse for a race horse! You worthless bag of horse bones!"

Up ahead, the Reverend Hardin had not slowed. If anything he was moving faster than before, set as he was into irresolution, the shotgun still waving wildly, threateningly, about his head. Behind him, the man on the winded horse came on, trying not so much to catch up as to stay in sight, yelling weakly, "Wait, Preacher! Wait!" expecting not to be heard, but if heard to be disregarded.

And there behind them both came the giant white dog, loping along like a great lugged bear, following in the path where the horse had just been, loping along and steadily losing ground.

Jim Stephens

Here I should back up and explain why John Wesley's father and mother and several other members of his family had moved from Mount Calm in Limestone County a hundred miles west to Comanche County to live. In those early days one part of Texas was not more desirable than another part where violence was concerned. All parts had their respective trouble. It was just different kinds of trouble, and the disadvantage in moving, as I now see it, was that you would be leaving the kind of trouble you were familiar with and had either overcome or adjusted to, only to relocate in another place which had its own kind of trouble so that you had to start over again and study it fresh.

At least a part of the move had to do with Wes's father and his wandering nature. Due to his training as a circuit riding Methodist preacher, he never felt comfortable in one place for long at a time. Over the years he came to acquire the vagrant look of a vagabond. Even when he would go to visit friends or relatives, they frequently would fail to offer him a chair. Too often they had seen him take his leave after staying only a few minutes, though he might have traveled half a day to get there. He also did not make friends easily nor did he have much success as a preacher. Somehow his congregations sensed he didn't have his mind on what he was doing or his heart in what he was saying.

Wes had a little of that vacant, abstract quality in him, as well. Hell, he had a lot of it, now that I think about it! That may have been one of the reasons he got in the trouble that he did. Trouble of some kind is always camped out in front of you, waiting for you to run into it. If you walk long enough in its direction, sooner or later you will find it. I guarantee it. Except for the misfortunate few, however, it will not repeatedly come where you are if you are content to stay in one place and settle down to an honest living. Of course, you must also learn to control your tongue as well as your desire to roam.

Take for example Wes's cousin Ira Lee High Pockets, a tall, frail figure of a man with no hips or butt to speak of. Over the years he provided Wes and me with a good deal of amusement as he could never manage to extricate himself from one fix without involving himself in a couple of others at the same time. Ira Lee acquired the nickname, High Pockets, from a persistent and annoying habit he had of pulling up his pants every few steps, a gesture he had acquired quite young. Apparently an uncle had once told him that simple friction and the natural effect of gravity would one day cause him to walk right out of his britches, and he believed it. More to the point, he never knew when to shut up or when enough was enough. Consequently, his mouth kept him in constant trouble, particularly with his wife. They had married late in their lives and seemingly out of futility and a fierce determination bordering on desperation—neither could stand himself. As it turned out, they couldn't get along with each other either, a development that had been expected, if not predicted.

No doubt the problem between Ira Lee and his wife was aggravated by the fact that both loved to talk, and each found the talk of the other insufferable. Over the years, this mutual dislike grew into casual, everyday hatred which they expressed at every opportunity, not only to each other but also to anyone else who would listen. Being an educated man, having taught school for several years in his early life, Ira Lee had somewhat of an advantage over his wife because of the numerous allusions and metaphors his education afforded him. What his wife lacked in an education, however, she more than made up for in intensity. Nevertheless, Ira Lee's smart mouth almost got him killed. He was lazing around the barbershop one afternoon, his hands periodically tugging up on the back of his pants, talking with a group of men whose current subject was wives and their faults. When it came Ira Lee's turn, he naturally chose as his subject his wife Bertha's "incessant and boorish talk."

Wes and I were in town that day so Wes could get his curly locks trimmed. This preening vanity was a monthly affair with Wes, as regular as the full moon, and he would not have missed it for anything, even for the chance to bet on a good horse race. As I have suggested before, Wes was a handsome man, and knew it. Much in the same way he took pride in his skill with guns, he took pride in his appearance, though this pride was in no way offensive.

Anyway, we were in the barbershop that afternoon, listening to Ira Lee talk about his wife.

"You can't really call what she has a mouth," he said, "just as you can't really call what comes out of it speech. The fact that it seems to set pretty much in the center of her face and to be continually spewing forth a curious blend of sound and heat is beside the point. Actually, what it resembles most is the fire-belching throat of an active volcano. It makes you want to get a rope and some spikes and climb up there and look in the way Caesar is reputed to have done at Vesuvius. Once there, however, you might be tempted to say, 'From here, it appears to be just another whore's mouth, though a little larger than most and a hell of a lot hotter!'"

When Ira Lee finished, Wes let out a horse laugh that could be heard all the way across the street. For him, such a response was out of character. Most men and their jokes did not amuse him, and the best I had ever seen him manage was a wry smile meant to acknowledge the cleverness of something that had been said without giving any credit to the humor of it. This is not to say Wes lacked a sense of humor. On the contrary, he had a fine, cultivated one, but it was reserved for the incongruities of life, the unexpected ironies that enrich a thinking man's day as well as his mind. He simply refused to acknowledge the banal, the mundane, the trite in human nature. It was another quality in him I greatly admired.

But it wasn't just Wes who was amused by Ira Lee's remarks. We all laughed when he finished, because we had never heard the case put in exactly that way. What none of us knew was that Bertha had been standing outside the door the whole time Ira Lee was talking. Instead of charging in and having it out with him on the spot, she went next door to the hardware store and persuaded the storekeeper to show her a new double-barrel shotgun and to demonstrate for her the way it was loaded. Then she asked to try loading it herself, but as soon as she got it in her hands, she ran out and positioned herself in front of the barbershop. Without a warning to anyone, except to call out her husband's name loud and quick, "Ira Lee High Pockets!" she discharged the first barrel through the largest section of plate glass in town, a fancy, ornamental art piece that had come specially etched and colored from somewhere back East. Later, she told the sheriff she only wanted to get it out of the way so she could have a clearer shot at her husband. The second barrel caught Ira Lee full in the chest as he was standing up brushing the broken glass out of his hair and off his clothes. What she didn't know was that she had shot the tight barrel first and the more open choked one second, so that the expanding charge caught not only Ira Lee but two other men including the barber. It all goes to show that you can talk yourself into trouble without going to the bother of looking for it.

Now, all this happened in Sumpter, and not in Comanche as you might expect, but if a fellow can't let well enough alone, it doesn't matter where he lives. Sooner or later, trouble will find him. That's the way it was with Wes back then, and that's the way it was with his father. I remember Wes saying he could always tell when his father had been in one place too long and was thinking about moving. He would never say anything to that effect, sometimes going for a month or more from the time he had made up his mind until he'd finally come out and say it was time to move. Usually, he would wait until everyone was gathered around the supper table to make what he always imagined to be an announcement of great surprise and one likely to be met with opposition. Much to his chagrin, that was never the case. His family always knew. They had learned to recognize the signs. He might start going to bed at night without taking off his clothes, not even his shoes, as though he were thinking of leaving first thing next morning. Or he would take off on long walks that might last for days and cover fifty or sixty miles round trip. Then one morning he would walk back into the yard with that Just Visiting expression on his face and a look of surprise in his eyes that his family was still there. It was as if he had expected them to follow him, bringing the wagons loaded with their possessions with the boys trailing along behind, tending the livestock.

For a week after such an announcement, Wes said, his father would walk around with a wounded look on his face as if he had been betrayed. Now in all the time I spent with the Hardin family, I never observed this phenomenon for myself, but Wes swears it was common. Whenever he told it, it always got a big laugh from the rest of the family, though Mr. Hardin did not find it amusing. He was sensitive about his wanderlust and would not speak of it.

A larger reason for the move out to Comanche County from Mount Calm, and for most of the other moves also, lay in the nature of the times. They were strange, sad times, lacking in security and contentment and not infrequently in joy and compassion while abounding in danger and violence. Had the men of that age been given the choice of living in some other span of time, past or future, many would have welcomed the choice, so intense were the sorrows and violence of those years and so pervasive the feelings of discouragement and futility. Perhaps I exaggerate, but I do not believe so.

Until their move to Mount Calm, the Hardins had lived in Trinity and neighboring counties for over ten years, but the unsettled times forced them to leave that area and eventually Mount Calm as well because they feared for their safety. In the early '70s, a curious blending of outlaws, defunct

Texas Rangers, and the infamous State Police had invaded even this central part of Texas, though they resided chiefly farther west and south in and around Gonzales and DeWitt Counties. This despicable group called itself the Vigilant Committee and was reputed to be on the side of law, order and justice while in fact it made those operations largely impossible, whereas before they had been only improbable. Life, liberty and property were in a constant state of jeopardy and uncertainty.

Unfortunately, such an organization was not uncommon in many parts of Texas during those years of radical reconstruction, although in moving out to Comanche County the Hardins felt they were beyond harassment at last. What they didn't realize or just didn't choose to see at the time and what it took me another year and the violent deaths of several of my friends and of my brother to realize was that their son John Wesley was responsible for a great many of their problems both in Gonzales County and particularly in Comanche County. No matter how fine and intelligent he was and in spite of a host of other good qualities, it was never his destiny to lead an easy life. He seemed to excite in other men, almost by instinct on their part, the same feeling that makes crows and hawks the natural enemies they are or more probably whatever makes men fear snakes and need to kill them when they get the chance. This instinct, if instinct it was, brought out in most men Wes encountered a meanness and a pettiness which they were a little embarrassed by afterwards, if they lived to tell about it.

Frankly, I am surprised that Wes lived as long as he did. I'm surprised that some good man somewhere acting for all men everywhere and for the simple protection, peace of mind, and well being of the race did not rise up in the name of indignation and common sense to shoot him in the back from the relative safety of a curtained window or some such place. But as I say, it took a long time for me to realize this feature about Wes and to recognize and identify in myself the vague uneasiness I felt in his presence, so strong was my need to be his friend and to aid him in abetting what on the surface and at the time seemed to me to be gross unfairness at the hands of almost everyone he made contact with. Even had his father not named him after the famous English preacher in whose wake the great religious wars of England and Scotland in the eighteenth and nineteenth centuries were said to have begun, it would have been the same. Upon such historical events, as thunder follows lightning, Mr. Hardin later tried to lay most of the blame for the way Wes turned out. By so naming his son, he felt he had in effect given the okay to fate to inaugurate a second such period of violence in this country, using for spark and impetus a second such figure much like the old one must have been in appearance and temperament. To his surprise, however, he discovered Fate had changed the essential characteristics in order to fit the reincarnation to a new land with new and different problems, thus changing a preacher into a gun man. Even when it was pointed out to him that conditions in Texas were what they were long before he moved there, much less engendered a son whose name would become an omen to all who heard it, Mr. Hardin persisted in his belief.

In truth, a thousand John Wesleys from the old mold and a thousand John Calvins thrown in for good measure would not have changed a thing. No doubt such men were even then in Texas and in just such numbers as they had been in the old country, only with different names and carrying guns now instead of Bibles, having discarded the muted message of one way of life for the more direct message of the other. I believe Mr. Hardin knew this, but he could not shake the guilt he felt in his misguided and unfortunate choice of a name. As he wisely and bitterly pointed out, only a fool deliberately throws a lighted match onto the dry prairie in the midst of a high, uncertain wind, that is if he values the sight of grass blowing or the mount on which he rides or even his own life.

However inaccurate that comparison, it was on the mark in one respect. Wes was definitely a match and every other man a potential striking surface, though lightning is a truer, more descriptive word, at least so to the men who went down before his gun.

In Comanche, Mr. Hardin apparently felt he had found a prairie too green to burn. There had been no organized citizen's action against lawlessness and violence in the county, other than vigilante action, since a group of local men had been formed to drive out the last marauding Comanche Indians in the late sixties. However, by 1874, unbeknown to Mr. Hardin, the mere mention of the name John Wesley Hardin anywhere within a hundred miles of the place was sufficient to draw some of the same men together in serious discussion. Though the word was out that an honest, god-fearing man had little to fear from Wes Hardin, fear and respect were mixed in proportions sufficiently unequal to encourage mob mentality, though such a possibility had not been discussed as far as I know. But as I say, in Gonzales County a mob already existed, and it was in no way Wes's doing.

Now this vigilant band was run by the sheriff of DeWitt County, Jack Helms, and his select group of deputies, most importantly Jim Cox, Joe Tomlison, and Bill Sutton. All were men of considerable reputation and proven ability both with a gun and with whatever other means of violence allowed them to do their work. They were feared from one end of the counties to the other, and no one spoke well of them. Only the strongest had dared stand up to them, and most came to regret that later on. Some of the most respected men in both counties had been murdered by this mob simply because they deplored the measures the mob was taking. One man, Pipkin Taylor, was tricked out of his house at night and in the moonlight, before the startled eyes of his wife and children, shot dead. This came about for no reason other than he had spoken out against the similar killings of his sons-in-law, Henry and Will Kelly. Another man, William Samuels, was taken out of his bed in the middle of the night and tied behind a horse and dragged across some of the roughest land in the county until he was dead. Next morning his body was found hanging from a sign post on the main street of Gonzales. It was speculated that he had been treated in this manner because he had refused to sell a horse he owned to one of the members of the committee a few day before his death.

In this manner the mob tried to intimidate people into accepting their lawless actions. I show you the times and ask how any strong-willed man of conscience and skill with a gun could have lived differently than Wes did or come to a different end. I also want to impress upon you the fact that lesser men than Wes, with less courage and less character, became petty and cruel in response to those times. Such was this mob and its leaders.

Julie Ola Faye

Shoooeeee, thank de Laud! Preacher Hardin done gone off to town for sho. Now I takes dese breasts out for a while and lets de wind blow over em.

"Here, Boy, you turns yo head. Dont you go lookin cause I bust yo bottom for sho."

Laudy, dat wind is so cool blowin like dat. If I jest had someone to hold dese tits up for me, some hands sides dese hands, Even dese feel so good to squeeze in on em. To pinch on em a little. Some men takes and twists on em and punch on em and suck on em and bite on em. But dere is some men wont hardly touch em. We likes men dat rough. A little.

"Boy, does you wants yo bottom spanked!"

Would you look at dat smoke now! Hit cant git no worse hit decided so hits gonna git better some.

"Okay, Boy, you turn round now. Here, put dis hoe in de wagon cause we gots to git home to dat hog like Preacher Hardin say. Fore it gits dark. I knows dat hog waitin for me. Hits sayin *"Whens dat old colored woman gonna git here cause I wanta gits killed soon as possible. I wanta be killed and et. I dont wanta be no hog no more."*

Hit aint no good. Hit will spoil. Hit wont last. Jest cause hits leg is bad dont mean hit has to be killed. Not if eatin hit will makes us all sick. Kill us too, most likely. Wid jest me here to take a stick and knock hit in de head spite what Preacher Johnny say bout dat gun.

"But my daddy say—" I says.

"Your daddy aint here," he say. "I'm here, and I'm telling you to use that gun!"

But my daddy never use nothin but a stick. He say dey die slower so dat de bloods still pumpin when you stick em in de neck. Dat way dey bleed more. After I gits him killed, I has to pull him up all by myself like I has to pull some of dose men up on dese titty mountains when dey too tired to climb up no more.

Jest likes I say to dat white man dat time.

"White man, you don't want dis ole nigger gal. You don't want no ole sinner like me. What you wants yoself be a nice clean white girl wid a white dress and white skin dat smells clean like flowers and wid hair like de sun. You dont want no ole sinner jest like Jesus dont want no ole sinner."

"Julie Ola Faye," he say. "I have seen Jesus and she is a pretty black nigger girl that saved the world by loving it. She saved all the men and all the boys just by letting them suck the love they needed right out of her big black tits. Now lie back there and put your legs up!"

"Yes, Masta."

Gots to git home and kill dat hog. Fore it gits dark.

"Come on here, Boy. If we gots to do hit, we gots to do hit, and dat ole white dog aint no better dan one of dem men runnin off like dat when he coulda helped us pull up dat hog. Hes bigger dan dat hog. He coulda helped us so much. But if you was to give him a gun, he be jest like de rest of dem men tryin to find somebody to kill wid hit.

"Come on, Boy, we gots to hurry."

If hit was jest me I walks into dat town and say *"I is here. Julie Ola Faye is here. She come to save her white boy dat sucked at de tit along wid his black brother. I too young den and too afraid to save my black boy, but I comes to save dis one. I dont care hes killed forty and jest killed five more. I aims to save him. I dont care hes jest burned down your town. Deres lots of towns. Now put down dose guns and uncoil dose ropes and put dat hate out of yo hearts cause I comes to save him with the weapon of love. I has plenty of hit to go round.*

Hits love he got suckin from de tit. Dey jest took him off too quick. Jesus say save dem wid love. Now hes killed forty men and maybe five more, but I saves him. Jest let me at him a minute. I suckles him once more from dis tit wid de gold ribbon, and den he lays down his six shooter and puts de hate out of his heart.

"*Den when dat done, dis ole white dog here gots more love dat I packed on him. Hes callin all sinners everywhere.*"

"Hurry now, boy. Lets run. Dem men be comin soon."

When dey donts find John Wesley, dey come like de fire in de night. But hit wont be night yet cept hit will be night in dere hearts, and dey will see me standin here naked as a jaybird bove dis boilin pot scrapin' de hair off dis ole hog. Cause I gots to give John Wesley more time. He finds him a place to hide if I helps him. So I jest pull off dis dress and stand here naked to git dem mens mind off John Wesley.

When dey see me, de hooves of dere horses flash fire like de preacher say and dey cry out *"There's Jesus. There's Jesus for sure."* Den dey takes me where I stand and throws me to de ground, and den dey casts lots for my love. One at a time dey will take dere fill of de love from dese ole tits. When dey finished, dey take a rope and puts me up dere side dat ole hog and head down over de pot. Oh laudy, poor ole nigger whore, but John Wesley be gone by den.

But first I needs to go to town.

"*Folks,*" I says, "*I didnt kill de hog dat was fatted on de corn cause hit couldnt git to de pasture no more on three legs. I comes here to town, Folks, and soon as I thru wid John Wesley here I gives some love to you all, and one ole sinful nigger whore takes all dat love and changes de world. I lays down here in de street and takes all you mens in turn wid you snuff and yo tobacco and yo rotted teeth and yo unwashed bodies and yo wrinkles and yo fat and yo bones and yo hands washed wid dirt, and I loves you all clean wid out havin' to spill no blood cause dats all John Welsey needs. Dats all he ever want. He jest lovin you wid his gun. He jest want to love you, and he do hit de only way he know to love you. Wid de bullet cause he cant love you yet wid his heart or wid his hands dat love only de gun."*

If I jest had dat ole white bear hound here dat loves to chew on de ears of dem bears. Dat ole white bear hound dat cant find no bears so he off to town see whats burnin jest like a worthless ole man would do. He could takes dat ole hog by de ear and drags hit up here so I woudnt have to lay out de corn from de barn lot to de tree. Wastin good corn jest to git him close to de pot. Least dont have to feed it no more, callin *"Here, Piggy, Piggy. Here, Piggy, Piggy, Piggy. Sooooeee, Piggy. Sooooeee, Piggy. Eat dis good corn."*

But dat ole dog is off actin like a man. Dat ole dog aint no bear, or he woulda stayed and helped.

Maybe I goes to town anyway no matter what Preacher Hardin say.

"Wait, White Folks," I tell em. *"Let dis ole nigger whore talk to John Wesley. Now you folks takes dat rope off his neck so he can talks back. I asks him for you what he bout."*

"Say, Boy," I tell J. W. Jesus. *"You boy dat is actin like dis, killin all dese forty men and maybe five more and burnin down folks town, you tell dese people who you are. Tell em like you tell yo Mama Julie."*

"Now, listen, Folks."

"Tell em, Boy."

"Why, Folks, I am John Wesley Hardin, and I am named after a famous preacher who spread blood and hate across Europe and England and called it the love of Jesus. My father is such a preacher now, and because of my famous name I have decided to become yet a third such preacher. But whereas my father preaches life eternal, I aim to preach death eternal. He uses water to baptise in the name of the Father, Son, and Holy Ghost. I use blood in the name of the ghost period! My father's message is love. He uses words to carry it forth. Mine is love too, and I use a Colt .44. I am John Wesley Hardin, great collector of souls for the Lord. Great grim reaper of the unjust and the unwise and the poor and downtrodden and the unloved. The anointed and christened savior of an entire

county. An entire state. The Promised One. And when it is over, when the last bullet is fired and the last man has fallen cold and dead and the last gun lies slender and shining in the cool white sand and even John Wesley Hardin will have been dead for a thousand years, then the new land and the new men will still be saying, Once upon a time there was a place called Comanche and once upon a time there was a John Wesley Hardin. Here he lived and here he died and here are the graves of the men he killed and these are their names and this grave here, this one that is set apart and lifted up is his own and once again after a thousand years glass everywhere will break and begin to fall. John Wesley is dead! Oh, weep, lost world. Weep for John Wesley Hardin who is no more.'"

"Now see, Folks, jest love like I tells you. Now let me suckle dis poor baby and him only fifteen and six mens dead already and three of em niggers, he says. And more even, he says."

"Boy, whats you tryin to do? Fight dat war all over agin?"

"Julie Ola Faye, you are the best nigger mammy I have ever had."

"I is de only nigger mammy you ever had."

How manys hit now? Now dat he twenty-one? Hit forty-five yet?

Dat ole white dog jest like de rest of em, but de way he sit back and look up at you and big as a horse and so wide on de back dat you could strap down yo saddle. I walks out de door sometimes, say "Here, Bear Boy. Here, Puppy Boy. Come on you ole bear hound, you."

At first, I dont know where he be. Out to de barn someplace or down off in de pasture. Den even fore I sees him, I knows hes a comin. Hits like puttin yo ear to de ground and listenin to de elephants walk in de jungle. Sometime I thinks I feel de earth shake, and den he come round de corner of de house waddlin like a bear.

"Hey, Lover Boy. Hey, Sweet Lover." So soft and white and thick. Masta Hardin say we oughta shear dat dog. He say dere more wool on dat dog dan on ten sheep. He say one shearin make a quilt. In de spring when all dat fur comin out, hits

like a walkin cotton field wid hit fallin off him all de time like hit rainin white bear fur.

But den sometimes he dumb like a man. Like he done today, runnin off to town.

"Here, Child, git up on dis wagon so we can go git hit done. Though hit will ruin. Hit wont keep."

I tells Preacher Hardin dat.

"You just do it," he say. "We will salt it and smoke it and with John Wesley and Jimmy here and Jane too that makes an even dozen of us. It won't last two weeks anyway."

Jest cause hit broke hits leg and gots to drag hit like a stick. Hit cant go off to de pasture wid de rest of em.

Laud, dese breasts needs some place to lie down. Some place dats cool. If dere was jest some hands comin round from behind to hold em up so dey wouldnt be so heavy.

If Preacher Hardin jest do his business and let me do mine. He think all us niggers needs to know is yes sir and no sir and yes maam and no maam and can I help you, maam, and what would you be wantin me to do today, Sir. He thinks we has babies and works in de cotton and has more babies and kills de hogs. Colored babies and half-white babies. He thinks we aint gots de sense to use a stick on a hog and not no ole gun so hit will bleed more and faster and longer.

You jest go on now, you ole preacher man. Let dis nigger woman kill dat hog de way her daddy taught her.

Dat smoke died down some, but I cans still kill hit and cut hit and string hit up fore dey come.

"Git up dere, you mule. You git up dere."

Dey comes jest like dey always do. Like dey did in Gonzales and like dey did in Sumpter fore dat. All of em ridin up to de porch.

"Where is John Wesley Hardin," dey say. "Where is that Jimmy boy? Where is Jim Taylor? Where is Manny Clements? Where are they? Tell us, or we will take this colored bitch out to the barn and let her tell us. Then maybe we will come back and get the rest of you women. Now where are them god damn sons of bitches. You tell them we got enough new ropes so they can all have one. Don't none of them have to use an old rope. You tell them that!"

And dese ole tits sittin up dere as pretty as you please, lookin out at all dem hands wantin to be up dere feelin round on dem cept I heard tell dey is meaner here in dis county. Dat dey jest hang who dey find if dey dont find who dey lookin for.

"Boy, when we gits to de house I wants you to gits yo pole and gits down to dat creek. You hear me! I wont need yo help wid dat ole hog. You jest gits in de way no how. You gits your pole and gits down to dat creek and catch you some grasshoppers and you sit dere and you fish till you catches nuff to feed us all for supper. You hear me, Boy! I dont wants to see you till full dark."

Hits four miles to de creek and four back. So when dey come, sayin, *"Nigger, have you seen John Wesley Hardin who has killed forty men and five more?"* dere wont be but one nigger here to hang. And no little nigger to watch what dey do fore dey use de rope.

"You use a gun," Masta say. "A gun is quicker. A gun is surer. If you use a gun, then you ain't gonna have it wake up on you where you are trying to cut its belly open so that you wind up cutting yourself instead of the hog. Or maybe it will wait until you have got it over the boiling pot, and then it will try to drown you."

But I aint gonna use no gun. I dont care whats dat white man say. Dat white man dont know nothin. John Wesley dont know nothin. Jimmy boy dont know nothin. Dey thinks cause dey got guns and can use de guns dat dey know somethin. My daddy say use a stick. Dat a good stick all any man ever need. My daddy say he knowed a man once dat never ate no food cept dat food he could shoot wid his gun. Papa say his pot always boilin full of dem squirrels and rabbits he shot wid dat gun and den one day he broke dat gun so hit couldnt shoot no more. Dat man say to Papa, "Nigger, aint you my friend? Wont you feed me out of your pot cause my gun done broke and I aint got me no food. I is starvin to death."

Papa say de man never had no money for nother gun.

Pretty soon his wife chase him out of de house wid a butcher knife, and den one day she gone. After a while dat man come back to livin in his house, and Papa taught him to use a stick so he never needed no gun. But till he learn he bout starve to death.

Dat smoke is less now. Dey be comin soon.

"Whoa, Mule! Whoa Mule! You gits down, Boy, and go on like I tells you. I turn loose dis mule and den I kill dat hog. Dis mule help me wid dat hog. You gits on now, Boy. Dont you come back till dat sun go down. Now git!"

Dey be here soon, askin,*"Where is that John Wesley Hardin, Nigger?"*

"Folks, let me ask him agin."

"John Wesley, Honey boy, why you kill people? Explain to dese good people here why you kill people."

"Why do I kill people? Why Mama Julie Ola Faye, I kill them because I like the smell of fear in a grown man as he stands trembling sweatless before a fifteen-year-old boy. I love the feel of the gun in my hand. I like the way it bucks when I pull the trigger. I am John Wesley Hardin. Boy killer. Lady killer. I command respect. I demand it. Give the right gun to me, I will rule the world. I teach men the lessons of life—to love God and their wives. To be kind to their children and their dogs. To walk upright and to work hard and with honest sweat all the days of their lives. And last, never to cross John Wesley Hardin."

"So men, he aint here," I says.*"You mens has to look some wheres else for what you want."*

But cause dey men and spite I be a nigger, dey see dese two ole pantin breats, and dey git to thinkin and pretty soon one of dem say, *"At least part of what we want is right here, Sheriff."*

And den dey laugh and den dey all start to git down. Dese two ole breasts see dat, and dey take no thought for my life. Dey will jest begin to reach out wid dose hands, and den if I holds out I gives John Wesley a couple more hours.

"Hold still, you mule!"

Dey is gonna kill me no ways cause I be John Wesley Hardin's nigger mammy. What I needs me is a dowsin rod. If I had me a dowsin rod, I find all dat gold folks says buried over dere on dat ole Round Mountain. Dat gold some folks say buried over dere on dat Sweetwater Creek where it run by de Round Mountain. What I needs is a dowsin rod. I gots to find me a peach tree somewheres so I can cut me a stick. A stick for killin de hog and a stick for dowsin up all dat gold.

Den I says, *"Here, Masta Johnny Hardin, here is all de gold we needs to move off some place where dere aint no trouble. We can take John Wesley too so he wont have to use dem guns."*

If I jest had me a good dowsin rod. I could do hit. If I cant find no peach branch, den I jest cut me a willow limb. A willow limb do hit for me. When I feels it shakin so I cant hold hit, turnin down on me so I cant hold hit, den I knows dere is de gold jest waitin for me to dig hit up out of de ground.

Dat smoke bout gone. "Git out of de way, mule, till I call you. I gots me a hog to kill."

Hits like dat dream I had. Like a vision. Hits all firey red rollin on wheels like a wagon. Fire into fire like de chariot of Eligah. Hit was rollin down de street. Den I look and see John Wesley and Jimmy boy hid out tryin to burn hit with fire. Dey breathin smoke into de smoke of the rollin fire. I cries out, "Hits the great and comin day of de Laud. De terrible day of de Laud. You boys cant kill hit wid jest fire. What is fire itself cant be kilt by no fire!"

Hits my dream. My vision. I first has hit years ago, and I has hit many times since. Hits a big red wagon rollin' on wheels pulled wid out mules, puffin fire and smoke and dem boys hid out tryin to kill hit wid fire.

Dis stick will do. Hits a good stout stick. A strong stick, and hit takes jest one blow like my daddy teach me.

When dey asks him, Masta Hardin say hits his fault John Wesley start like he did.

"I accept the blame," he say. "If I just hadn't named him after that preacher. If I had just given him a normal name like other people have, then he wouldn't always be trying to prove himself the way he does. He has always had to live two lives. The one I gave to him was already lived up with deeds and history, and the other one was his own. The one I gave him was always trying to crowd out the one that was his own by right of birth. So he felt he had to show people that there was a Hardin attached to the end of that John Wesley that made him different than the other John Welsey that had the deeds and the history."

"Masta Johnny," I says, "why didnt you jest name him Jesus Christ Hardin?"

Sayaaaa, but aint hit hot now for one ole nigger whore to be workin like dis. Dis sweat needs to blow cool in de wind cross my parts and since hits jest me, I will. If I dont pull dis dress off, I gits blood all over hit. I lets down dese two tits dat men cants keep dere hands off of and let de wind blow cool through my parts.

Like dat night Jesus say, "You leave yo window unlatched."

First, I pulls off my clothes and stands naked in de dark of de room and den I opens de window and goes back and lays out on de bed open to de wind and de moon and de stars.

I say, "Whatever come thru dat window, I jest cant stop hit."

Dis here stick sho a good one. Hits big enough, and hits long enough, and dat ole hog jest be standin dere eatin on dat corn, and den I hits him right in de center of de head. Right tween de eyes. He stands dere for a minute and say to himself, *"Dis ole nigger woman done hit you wid a stick, and you dead."*

Den he fall over, and I takes de knife and cuts his throat. Den I takes de stick and throws hit away and gits de gun and sets hit here by de tree. No, I shoots hit in de head first so Preacher Johnny say what a good job I done.

Laudy, dat evenin wind is cool. I jest hang dis here dress on dis nail, and after I washes de blood off nakid body, I puts hit back on.

And me jest fourteen cause Papa dont like no creamy niggers comin round sayin, "I is a good man. I aint never been in no jail. I is worth a thousand dollars cause I is a good worker, and I is worth a thousand more cause I aint dark likes you. I like to marry dis here gal. She has dem big tits dat needs somebody creamy like me to hold on to em so dey wont git lonesome."

Right dere on dat nail so dey sees hit hangin up and knows I aint tryin to hide no gun under it, sayin to me, "Where is that gun you used to kill that hog with, since we can see it aint on your body?"

"I dont use no gun. I use a stick."

"Then, why does it have a hole between its eyes?"

"I still dont use no gun."

And all de time I gots dese pistols of John Wesleys hid up in de belly of dat ole bleedin hog.

And Mama say, "God strike you dead out of de storm cloud. Here, come wid me to de preacher so he cans give you de care you need. De cure you need."

What if hits ten of dem men lookin for John Wesley? What if deres more? How long dat take wid dat ole hog hangin up dere all de time bleedin and me naked to de sun like dis and dese breasts reachin out to all dose hands? What if hits a hundred?

Mama say, "Laudy, you a sinful nigger. Jesus Christ dont want no sinful nigger like you. You de sinfulest nigger I ever knowed. When de Laud strikes you dead and dey puts you in de ground, you gonna sprout sin jest like a potato grow eyes."

And I jest lays dere in de dark and lets come in de window whats comin in de window, and when hit gots in de bed wid me, hits hands got on to dese breasts and hits mouth say, "Is all dis for little ole me?" and it lays dere and rolled and sucked and squeezed and rolled and sucked and squeezed some more.

"—and sprouts come up jest like a potato. You de sinfulest nigger I ever knowed. We gots to git you to a preacher."

Dis stick sho nuff do. Dat ole broken leg hog aint gonna run. First, I gots to git hit some corn to gits him over here under dis limb. But first I has to git some fire goin under dis pot like in de vision. Take a whole wagon load of cotton and spread hit round dat firey red wagon, runnin long like dat wid a metal heart and metal face and ears and eyes. Gots to do hit so John Wesley and Jimmy boy cans fire de cotton wid me standin dere tellin em, *"You boys cant kill with fire what eats fire. Hit will jest eat de fire too."*

Jest like I couldnt save my black boy from de law though de black ones on one tit and de white ones on de other tit, suckin almost like hands. When I was grievin, I lies in bed wantin my black boy back, thinkin how maybe my daddy was wrong a little when hit come to guns. How my colored boy try to beat off de law with a stick and it wont work. How for takin what he did out of dat store de law comes and git him, stick or no stick. But John Wesley here take a gun and hold off a whole town of law. So my daddys right and hes wrong. You needs a stick for hogs and a stick for findin gold and water, but for robbin' a store and killin men you gots to git yoself a gun.

Dats why dem mens be comin any minute now, lookin for John Wesley.

Now dat oughta be nuff wood to fire hit and start carryin in de water. Now wheres dat bucket? If John Wesley jest here to help wid carryin dis water.

He say, *"Mama Julie Ola Faye, let me do that for you."*

And I be shamed for him to see me like dis wid dese two breasts pointin out dis way. But Jimmy boy could. I lets him if he jest here. He done seen em before. Oh Jesus, come quick and help dis ole nigger whore. Now wheres dat bucket?

Jimmy boy done help John Wesley burn down de whole town of Comanche. He lyin out dere in de street now tryin to git hisself shot. I be waitin for de glass to start fallin all over de world cause John Wesley Jesus dyin, but dere was no glass in dat window, jest boards. So I undid de latch and left hit open for Jesus and jest lay back on de bed, waitin and me jest fourteen.

Oh, laudy, if I jest had dem fancy ribbons my mama made me for all dese hands dats ridin hard to git here wantin me to save em wid my love.

Jim Stephens

The Gonzales mob was almost two hundred strong by the time Wes and I first encountered them. As an example of the mob's behavior and of the authority it felt itself to have, allow me to relate our initial meeting with Jack Helms. Although we did not suspect it at the time, the meeting was a prelude to numerous other meetings with Helms and his gang that would occupy our time for some months and might have beyond that had we not moved the center of our cattle and farming operation from Gonzales to Comanche. Ironically, we made the proverbial jump from frying pan to fire. There in that small frontier town we were to discover the same old, waiting trouble of which I have spoken but which this time around clearly signaled the end for Wes and for our association. I often thought about Wes after the doings in Comanche were finished, and occasionally I read about him and met and talked with mutual friends who had been with him in that early time, but I was never to see him again.

All in all, the break with Wes was much easier than I had ever imagined it could be. I will not pretend I had not thought about a parting of the ways, but once it came it brought relief beyond anything I had hoped for. For the first time in years I was able to sleep at night without fear of who might be coming up on me in the dark. Being able to take a job and associate with everyday people was a pleasure I had not experienced. It's strange that I could leave someone who had been close to me and important in my life and not feel any more than I felt. I could never explain it. I don't try any more. Though there would be many days and nights when I would sorely miss what I had with Wes, I never regretted my decision to leave, and I doubt he gave it a second thought. That was his way. I will admit, however, that I was somewhat disappointed when I first discovered that he had made no mention of me in the autobiographical account of his life. It was as if I had never existed and the experiences I had with him all a fiction I had concocted in my head. Whether he made the omission out of spite because I had broken with him or to protect me that I might settle down into an ordinary life, I will never know.

But getting back to the subject—the meeting with Jack Helms went like this: at the time Wes and I were making plans to leave the neighborhood where he had decided to set up a house for his wife and to travel to Cuero about twenty-five miles distant, since it was the nearest railroad and we had business to conduct there connected with the shipping of our cattle. Wes had earlier said how he wished to establish a home for his wife and future children and to build up a little cattle trade so he wouldn't have to depend on gambling for his spending money. As much as any man, he was aware of the passions that pastime aroused in people, and he wanted to put the practice behind him, as his father had often urged him to do. It was his further wish that I make my home there with him and Jane until I had found a wife of my own.

Early in the morning of the day we were to set out, a man by the name of John Gay came to see Manning Clements, an old friend who was staying with the Hardin family, to discuss a new road that was to be opened up from Cuero to San Antonio. The road would run not far from Clement's house, and according to Gay it was destined to become the major roadway of that region and as such would be of importance to those who lived either on it or nearby. It was Gay's plan that he and Clements work together to persuade those in charge of laying out the road of the advantage of running it through their places.

When Gay learned of our destination, he said he had just come from Cuero and if we would but follow his furrow back across the prairie we could save time and be less likely to encounter one of the small groups of vigilantes scouring the county looking for people to intimidate and mistreat. It sounded like a good plan and fitted in exactly with the kind of anonymity Wes wanted to maintain in Gonzales County until he had established himself as a law-abiding citizen.

After breakfast, Wes and I said our goodbyes and rode out. For the first couple of hours, we went along without incident, finding the furrow fully as clear and straight as Gay had told us it would be. However, when we were about eighteen miles from home and opposite the Mustang Mot, we saw a man riding on a large gray horse moving parallel to us and about two hundred yards distant. He appeared to be following us, and Wes remarked that he was heavily armed. We could see twin six shooters hanging from the saddle horn and a Winchester rifle cradled across one arm. When he saw we had spotted him, he turned off to the side and got down from his horse, apparently to make us believe he had no interest in our persons or in what we were doing in that part of the county. What he was really doing was dismounting so he could get a steady shot at us. Wes recognized this ploy, so we also reined up and got down beside our horses as if we were checking their shoes. On seeing this, the man mounted again and continued on his way.

"Who is he?" I asked. "What's he up to, anyway?"

"Either he knows who we are and means to kill us or he doesn't and simply isn't taking any chances," Wes said. "Either way he has bought himself some mighty expensive trouble."

Never one to forgo curiosity, especially when it involved a chance to use his gun, Wes suggested we go over and ask directions as a way of ascertaining the man's intentions.

"Howdy, Friend," Wes said as we rode up.

The man raised his left hand in greeting but did not speak. Upon closer inspection he proved to be a larger man than he had appeared at a distance. Everything about him seemed unnecessarily big—his head, the features of his face, his chest, his hands, and so on until he became to my eyes a comic figure.

Wes went on.

"My partner here and myself are traveling from San Antonio to Cuero and have been told this furrow will take us there. Can you tell us how far that is?"

Wes asked his question so matter of fact that curiously I found myself wanting to hear the answer, forgetting for the moment what it was we were trying to determine. It had the same effect on the man, taking him off his guard.

"About seven more miles," he replied. He then went on to explain that he was sheriff of Gonzales County and that he had been to serve papers on a man who lived nearby. He had thought we might be friends of the man, wanting to do him some harm.

It was as if the man had played one card and then on second thought decided to play another. Either he felt we were no threat to him or we were, in which case he had better establish himself and post his credentials. What he didn't know was that his opponent in the game—and a game it had become—was quite formidable himself. From there on, it was a pleasure to watch Wes take him down.

"I suppose your name is Dick Hudson," Wes said next, as we had heard that a man by that name was sheriff.

"No, Dick is my deputy," the man informed us. "My name is Jack Helms."

"I'm John Wesley Hardin," Wes said, and the mention of the name had exactly the effect Wes knew it would have. Helms's hand tightened on the rifle he was holding, and a dull cold film settled over his eyes. Then he came to himself and offered his hand.

Instead of taking it, Wes gave him a challenge.

"Now is your chance to take me to Austin," Wes told him. "We are man to man and face to face, on equal terms. You have said I was a murderer and a coward and have had your deputies after me. Now arrest me if you can. I dare you to try it."

Wes had him beaten, and Helms knew it. It was a curiosity to see such a man as Helms back down, as he was used to having his way where other men were concerned. Only one step remained in his humiliation, and all along Wes and I had seen that as the object of the game. Before he would be satisfied, Wes wanted to see Helms beg for his life.

"Wesley, I am your friend," Helms said then, "and my deputies are hunting you on their own account and not mine."

Wes had his pistol out by now.

"You are armed," he said to Helms. "Defend yourself. You have been going around killing men long enough, and I know you to belong to a legalized band of murdering cowards and have hung and murdered better men than yourself."

To this Helms replied, "Wesley, I won't fight you, and I know you are too brave a man to shoot me. I have the governor's proclamation offering $500 for your arrest in my pocket, but I will never try to execute it if you will spare my life. I will be your friend."

In his fear, Helms had let the rifle slip out of his hand and fall to the ground. With that, Wes had seen enough. Now that all resistance was gone, the game was no longer enjoyable.

After several more minutes of conversation in which Wes informed Helms that he would hold him responsible for his deputies' actions, we separated, promising to meet next day in Cuero and come to a formal understanding about the governor's warrant.

Wes and I went on to Cuero, tended to as much of our business as we could that day, and took a room at the hotel for the night. The next day we met Jack Helms as scheduled and again talked for some minutes, after which we separated, agreeing to meet later on the 16th of the month. This second time around, Wes talked to Helms man to man, according him his dignity as a person although he had little regard for him as a man. Still, even in this, it was a move calculated to put Helms at the most disadvantage and ourselves at the least. However peaceful this particular meeting with Jack Helms and the trip in general so far, Wes and I were not destined to leave Cuero that day without trouble. Again I show you the times.

After Wes and I finished our business in town, we entered a bar on the southwest corner of the square and took a drink with friends. Then we were shown into a back room where a poker game of several days duration was going on, and there we joined in on the play at the first opportunity. Before we had time to play one hand through, a man by the name of J. B. Morgan rushed up to us and insisted on buying Wes a drink. He'd heard Wes was in town and that he had single-handedly backed down Jack Helms and his mob. It was a generous offer, even friendly, but the man was drunk and belligerent in his manner. He demanded we get up then and come out to the bar and did so with such command and show of authority that he made himself unwelcome to all present. When Wes refused him, Morgan got mad and wanted to fight. He was a large framed man, somewhat over weight, and thus had reason to feel confident he could handle himself against Wes, who by comparison seemed frail. The first move he made was to knock most of the playing cards onto the floor. This, of course, broke up the poker game, and while some of our friends held Morgan back, we walked out and went on about our business. We soon forgot about Morgan, but later in the day, just as we were about to leave town, he came over to us and said to Wes, "You have insulted me, and I must fight you. Are you armed?"

"I am," Wes told him, "but I do not want to fight you."

It was an uncharacteristic move for Morgan to take, we were informed later, and a foolish one, also. He was not a professional gun hand, and he lacked wide experience in dealing with men. Wes had seen this in the saloon, and that is the reason he left without a fight. But Morgan was not to be denied.

"Well, it is time you were defending yourself," he said, beginning to draw his pistol. Before he could get it clear, Wes pulled his .44 and fired, the ball striking Morgan just above the left eye. He immediately fell dead, and we went on to the stable for our horses. As there had been several witnesses to what had taken place, we were allowed to leave town unmolested.

Our next encounter with Jack Helms was a direct result of this killing of J. B. Morgan. About the 23rd of April 1873, he and fifty of his men came into our neighborhood, inquiring for Wes, Manning Clements, Jim Taylor, and myself. When he learned we were not present, he became rude and insulted the women folk. He was especially rude to Wes's wife because she would not inform him as to where he could find either ourselves or any of the Taylors, who were good friends of the Hardins. It seems that back around the first of April Jim Taylor had shot Bill Sutton, a friend of Helms. Although he had not killed him, the mob was out to get the Taylors and all their friends. It was such action as this involving the women that the mob had engaged in for well over a year, always picking on the defenseless and singling out men and killing them while giving them little or no chance to defend themselves. The women were lucky that day since Helms and his mob had reportedly raped and killed two other women previous to that time. Perhaps they thought we were close by and were thus afraid to take that chance.

After we came in that night and learned what had taken place, Wes got hold of the Taylors and some of their friends, and we determined the mob would stop this kind of harassment or pay the consequences for their actions. A fight came off not long afterwards, around the 15th of May 1873, in which Jim Cox, one of the leaders of the vigilant committee, and another man, Jake Christian, were killed. The fight resulted in a complete rout of the mob, its members having no taste for anything resembling a fair exchange. Although Wes was popularly credited with killing both men, the mob still assumed the killings were at the urging and direction of the Taylors, who—it was believed—had contracted Wes to do their business only because they were afraid to do it themselves. Thus was the character of our sojourn in Gonzales County despite our determination to live peacefully and set up our home there. However, we were to have one more run-in with Helms before we left that country for good.

On the 16th of May, Wes and I, along with Jim Taylor, went to the little town of Albukirk in Wilson County according to our agreement. Once again we were to talk seriously with Jack Helms and some of his friends, their thinking being that by offering Wes a place of leadership in the mob they could persuade him to come over to their side. Failing that, they thought to offer him and his family constant protection in exchange for non-interference on Wes's part. These overtures to Wes grew out of a simple logic. The mob knew if Wes threw in with the Taylors he could single-handedly turn the tide against them. They would offer him almost anything to prevent that happening. Although this approach must have seemed a good plan to Helms and the mob, they were assuming Wes to be like themselves. He was not, as I have tried to point out.

When we reached Albukirk that day, it was decided that Jim Taylor would not attend the meeting. As there were many hard feelings between Jim and the mob, Wes and I went on alone. We met with Helms for over two hours that morning but failed to reach an agreement, and upon parting Helms threatened Jim Taylor's life. He was obviously angry, as well he might have been. He had offered Wes virtually unlimited license to come and go as he pleased in Gonzales County and had had his offer flung back in his teeth. For the second time, he had seriously misjudged his adversary, something not many men then alive could boast of.

After the meeting, Wes and I went to Jim Taylor and told him Helms had sworn to shoot him on sight. Because he had shot Bill Sutton and was a Taylor, he was no longer safe in the county of Gonzales. Jim then asked us to point out Helms to him since he had never had dealings with him directly but only through his subordinates. This Wes refused to do.

We then went to the blacksmith shop where Wes's horse was being shod and stood talking to the smith and watching him work. Meanwhile, Taylor went off to find Helms. As the smith was finishing with the shoeing, we saw Taylor coming back up the street, not having had any luck locating Helms. We had just paid for the shoeing when we heard Helms's voice.

"Hands up, you damn son of a bitch," he said.

We looked around and saw Jack Helms coming up on Jim Taylor with a large knife in one hand and a gun in the other, evidently meaning to disarm him and then kill him with the knife. He was larger than Taylor and might have done it too, but what surprised me was that Helms hadn't shot Taylor as soon as he saw him. That action would have been consistent with his behavior toward other men over which he had had an advantage. (I remind you of our first meeting with Helms and his intentions toward us at that time.) We later decided that Helms didn't feel the need to shoot Taylor on sight, not only because he was bigger than Taylor but also because he had taken him by surprise. Upon further reflection, it seemed as plain that Helms had not seen Wes where he stood inside the shadows of the shop.

Just then, someone across the street yelled, "Shoot the damned scoundrel!"

At that point Wes grabbed up his shotgun, stepped through the door, and fired a charge of buckshot into Jack Helms's chest. Later, he told me he did it because it seemed to him that Helms was the scoundrel, although the man who yelled was one of Helms's friends and had meant that Jim Taylor be shot. From my vantage, it looked as though Wes gave Helms more than enough time to use his gun had he wanted to. It is my opinion that Helms simply did not believe Wes would shoot him. It was his third misjudgment, and it cost him his life.

While Wes was occupied in holding off Helms's friends, Taylor walked over to where Helms lay on the ground and shot him several times in the head. It was an unnecessary act since Helms may already have been dead or most certainly would have died, but then Helms had murdered several of Taylor's friends, including his uncle, for no reason I could discover. I can understand why Jim did it.

The killing of Jack Helms marked the beginning of the

end of mob violence in Gonzales County, and Wes received many congratulations for his part in bringing it to an end. By this time, however, the Hardin family had moved out to Comanche County, and Wes had sent his young wife along too, fearing for her safety any time he left her alone. He was correct in making this move, since several more outbreaks of violence occurred before the good citizens of the county finally worked out an agreement which effectively stopped the killings.

In the meantime, Wes and I started to work cattle again, and between roundups, we made a couple of trips to Comanche to visit the family. On the last of these, Wes bought the race horse Rondo from Mavis Ansley, a young farmer who lived northwest of town on a small farm where he raised cotton and watermelons. As I recall he had an uncommonly pretty wife. This was the same Mavis Ansley who was to get himself killed some fifteen years later by one of the Caywood boys in an argument over a fence which kept Caywood's cattle from watering along the creek.

Wes and I continued to work cattle in and around that area, and on the 5th of May 1874, we traveled some twenty miles into Brown County to get a herd of cattle we had bought and were started back with them when it became evident we would not reach Comanche before night. Rather than risk losing our herd in the dark, we elected to stay over at Mrs. Waldrup's, a well-known stopping point on the major cattle trail through that area. That night around the supper table she related how one Charley Webb, a deputy sheriff of Brown County, had been to her house and arrested her son and had cursed and abused her. It was the first time we had heard the name of the man Wes was to shoot down outside a Comanche saloon some three weeks later, but however regrettable Webb's behavior seemed to us that night and however typical it would have been for Wes to drop everything and go off in search of this Webb with the intent of forcing an apology out of him, we felt we could not leave the cattle and must push on to the railhead several miles northwest of De Leon, if we were to meet our deadline.

The next morning Wes and I drove our cattle into Comanche. In the brief time we were there, before moving the cattle on north, Wes contracted to run his horse Rondo and two other horses, Shiloh and Dock, in two races to be held at the Comanche track on the 26th of May, 1874. By ironic coincidence, Wes's 21st birthday also fell on this date.

Julie Ola Faye

Wheres dat corn now dat I gots de wood up under de pot? Wheres dat corn? Wheres de bucket for de water? If you don't hurry, ole nigger woman, dey is gonna come ridin down dat road. If you hads sense, you would git on dat mule and go over to de creek and pick up dat boy. Den you both ride to dat ole Round Mountain and hide out. If you hads sense. Wheres dat bucket?

But I caint think bout dis hog for thinkin bout all dose hands dats comin like de hands in Sumpter and de hands in Gonzales. But dis time dey kill you, you ole sinnin nigger whore. Not even two such fine tits can make up for de burnin of a whole town.

"Here, Piggy. Here, Piggy, Piggy. Come git dis good corn."

Wheres dat pig?

"Soooeee, here, Piggy, Piggy."

Wheres dat corn?

"My poor John Wesley Hardin boy. Oh Johnny. Oh Johnny, why donts you come home to yo Mama Julie? Yo poor lost sweet nigger mammy who sits in de wind somewheres on de rocks long de edge of de world and cries in sadness. In loneliness. Why donts you come home? Lay down dose guns and come home to dem dat loves you. Come home where yo poor sweet lost nigger mammy waits in de dark for her brown haired boy and her black haired boy and waits for whatevers lost and whatever needs love and whatevers comin in de window. Glass or no glass.

"Oh John Wesley Hardin. So what if you lives dat long So what if you lives dat lucky? So what if you searches out all de men everywhere who is unjust and unlovin and you converts them to love and to death and to de grave and to hell? So what den?"

"Why then, Mama Julie Ola Faye, I will surely die. The Lord will call me home to my reward, and when I have breathed my last, my followers will cast down their coats upon the ground and throw down flowers in the path of those who bear my bones to their final resting place, and the sound of mourning will be so great that glass everywhere will begin to break and fall until the sound of shattering, falling glass will disturb the whole world and all the stars that lie above it."

"Weep, oh World. John Wesley Hardin is dead. He came to love you from afar, and when he preached, a church that held ten thousand was never big enough and the sound of his voice was as the sweep of angels wings and of the crack of thunder, and lo he came out of the wilderness clad only with a .44 and baptised forty and five more in the name of the Lord of Hosts by the time he was twenty-one years of age. Blessed be the name of the Lord!"

Masta say, "We will all be home to help you cut it up and salt it and hang it in the smoke house."

But hit wont make no difference. I tells him hits gonna ruin fore we git hit put up. Hits too hot in May to kill no hog. Jest cause hit turned off cool dont make no difference. And jest for a day or two no way. Hit wont stay cool. Sides, hit aint dat cool. But de wind blowin de sweat off dese breasts is so sweet and so cool.

Den de smoke come risin out of de roof of that ole smokehouse. Pourin out of de cracks in de boards thick as clouds and out round de door like hits so full of smoke hits bout to crack open like a sour watermelon. Jest waitin to crack down de side like in my vision wid de smoke puffin out of dat red wagon dat aint made of no wood, sittin dere in de middle of de street burnin cotton, jest laughin at dem boys tryin to burn hit up.

Masta say, "After it has smoked some, we will cook up a big batch of it for supper tonight. There will be an even dozen of us. It won't have time to ruin. You be sure you save us them brains to eat with our eggs."

Hit wont make you no smarter. Hit wont make John Wesley no smarter neither. He done had em fore now and he still use dat gun. If you eats brains, you should act like you eats brains. Mama say I eats too many chicken hearts when I was little. Dats why I gots so much love. But brains is to make you smart.

John Wesley say fore he left dis mornin, "You put them brains in a pan of hot water for a minute and then you take them out and put them in a pan of cold water and then in the morning scramble them in the eggs for me. I love them that way."

So do Mama Julie, Honey Child. Dem eggs and brains is so good! But dis ole nigger woman wont be fixin em.

One, two, three, four, five of dem buckets of water from de well. I jest needs me five more. Den I gits dat ole hog over here to eats dis corn so I can kill hit. Honey Child, cause you is a nigger, you had to hunt up de wood and draw de water and start de fire and den kill de hog and you all neckid like a jay bird bendin down over dat well for de water. ONE. Lettin dem two breasts hang down for a look. Hits a good thing dis well so close to de tree and de pot. TWO. But you cans jest draw water to boil. You caint put out no fire wid water you has to draw from a well. THREE. Dere jest wouldnt be no way like in de vision. You caint fight fire wid a horse dat eats fire and breaths fire and rolls on iron wheels and has on iron feet and wears an iron face. FOUR. If you heaps all de cotton in de world and sets hit on fire, hit jest eats that too and keeps right on comin after you. FIVE.

Phewee, dats all de water. Phewee, hits hot.

"Here, Piggy. Here, Piggy, Piggy. Drag yoself up here under dis rope. Right over here side dis pot dat is beginnin to boil so I can hits you in de head wid my stick. So I can scramble yo brains like eggs wid dis ole stick."

Dis ole nigger woman aint gonna be eatin dem brains neither cause dey gonna climb down off dem horses where I is standin dere wid out no clothes on and dese two breasts will start reachin for all dem hands. Laudy, laudy, you is gonna git us killed for sho, for sho. But maybe dey aint gonna like you wid all dis sweat on you. Maybe dey will jes turn up dey noses and say,"*We aint gonna root around like hogs sucking on those two old sweaty tits.*"

Shoooeeee, its hot. I dont care how cold Preacher Hardin say it is, hits gonna ruin. Hit will spoil and den we all takes sick and die. I sho do wish I hads me some good fresh chitlens fore I git killed. I know dey is gonna kill me. I knows you caint have yo chitlens no matter how much you love em cause you caint burn down a town like dat. You jest caint. You caint burn down no red wagon neither dat is already fire. Metal wont burn. Hit jest gits hot and red and burns you up.

Oh Laudy, some chitlens boiled and cut up and rolled in de butter and fried. Fore dey is thru wid me, layin me down here in de sand on my back wid my knees lifted up and one at a time all twelve of em and all of em standin dere watchin right under dis hog wid de blood drippin off both of us. Me all spread out like dat and all de world starin at my parts cause I gots all dat love to give dat is gonna save John Wesley and Jimmy Boy jest like Jesus had all dat love and he give some of hit to me. Wid dat ole hog hangin dere upside down jest watchin us like his head floatin in de boilin pot gittin ready for de souse meat.

"Here, Piggy. Here Piggy, Piggy, eat dis nice corn."

Okay, jest hit him once now. Jest one quick one like my daddy say right dere tween de eyes while he lookin down at de corn.

Whop!

Pheweee, dat not so bad. Jest one blow. Ah oh! Laudy, nigger. My, my, my! Lookiee at him kick round on de ground, ole woman. Dese tits got in de way or he be dead. Whop him agin, nigger.

Whop! Whop! Whop!

Good thing dat preacher man aint here. He say, *"I told you to use that gun! I told you to forget about that stick!"*

Now, nigger woman, git dat rope on him quick so you can stick him in de throat. Git de rope on him so you can put on de block and de tackle and haul him up. Why, deres dat mule still at de barn.

"Come here, mule! Heauhie, mule. Heauhie, mule. Come eat dis good corn. Dis ole hog dont want hit no more. Now, heauhie, mule! Heauhie, mule!"

Stick him, woman. Git de blood to runnin.

"Come here mule. Good boy. Come here."

Laudy, lookiee at dat mule run. Lookiee at him kicks his heels up. My daddy say, "Lookiee dere. De ole horse fly done bit dat mule right on de back."

"Jimmy crack corn and I donts care. Jimmy crack corn and I donts care. Jimmy crack corn and I donts care. My mastas gone away.

"Here, mule, eats dis good corn fore de blood run out all over hit. Eat hit now and be still, damn you, while I puts dis rope on. Whoa, boy. Now, pull, mule. Now pull up, damn you!"

Mama say, "A knife in de gut. No, dats a bullet in de gut, gal. Bout de same thing as a hand reach in to pull all yo stomach out. So you lets him play wid you, you hear! You be nice to him up dere in de big house. You do hit so you wont has to works in de field no more. You cans make yo mama proud of you."

"Oh, I'm gonna lay down my sword and shield down by de river side. Down by de river side. Down by de river side. I'm gonna lay down my sword and shield down by de river side. Down by de river side.

"You can eats dat blood and corn later, mule. Now pull up. I mights as well wait till de sun go down as to waits on you. You aint gonna move till all dat corn gone, jest like a fool ole man!

"Nobody knows de trouble I've seen. Nobody knows but Jesus. Nobody knows de trouble I've seen."

When my baby boy Wesley was fifteen and hit was four

men killed, I asked Masta Hardin, "Why he kill like dat?"

"Because he is young yet," Masta say. "Because he must find himself first. Because he flees the call of the Lord, but soon now he will surrender. Soon now, he will lay down his gun and take up the holy word of God, and he will no longer kill men. He will save them, and his name will be spoken, but now the Hound of Heaven pursues him and he would flee to the depths of darkness. Now he is wounded and afraid and woe to all men who stand in his path. But one day soon he will be raised up and the coal of fire be placed on his tongue, and he will lay down his gun and pick up his Bible. It will be as if Christ lived again. Praise the Lord!"

"Dat is de truth, Folks. Lookiee how he takes dis love at de tit. He loves you people. Stand back now. Uncoil dat rope from dat tree. Take dem guns down and puts de love back in yo mouth. He all most thru now and hit be all yo turns. I suckle all you. I gives you de love Jesus gave me."

"Nobody knows de trouble I've seen. Nobody knows but Jesus. I'm gonna lay down my sword and shield down by de river side, down by de river side, down by de river side. I'm gonna lay down my sword and shield down by de river side cause my mastas gone away."

If I jest had dat ole worthless dog dat thinks hes got to run off to town jest like a damn fool man to see whos shot and whats burnin. If I was a smart nigger, if I hads any sense, I puts a saddle on dat ole white dog and rides off to meet Jesus in de air. But dese tits knows all dose white hands comin dat needed all dat love. But you cans rides a bullet in yo belly same as you cans a dog and faster too.

When John Wesley was a baby, his mama looks into his face and say, "This boy of mine is going to break women's hearts."

She meant wid his love. She didnt know hit would be by killin dey men folks.

Dere is a wind comin up. I feels hit jest like I always does. I hears hit beginnin to blow thru de trees down below de house. I hears hit whislin round de sides of dat ole Round Mountain fixin to blow hot and steady out of de southwest jest like I told Preacher Hardin. Hits too hot for no hog killin but when you is a nigger and a white man tells you somethin you does it.

"Come on now, yo sweet thing you, so I cans git my hands on dem breasts," what Mama say he meant. "Why don't you come on up to de house wheres its cool. Maybe I can finds some work for you to do."

Dat boy, dat John Wesley boy has done gone and burned down a whole town so dat ole bear hound has to go in and see whats burnin like a darn man.

"Holds still, mule, while I ties dis rope!"

I says to Wesley, "Dat old white bear hound is yo friend now but he wont always be yo friend. He was followin dat red wagon in my vision, runnin long side of hit, and if you and Jimmy tries to burn hit, he eats on you. He crawls up on top of you and eats out yo throat jest like you was a bear."

Dat wind is comin. Hits blowing so cool on dese parts. Hit will rain slow tonight but first hit will come a gully washer and wipe de blood of dis hog off de ground and off de place where dis ole nigger woman lays down in de dirt.

"Now all you mens git down off dem horses. Sheriff, tells em to git down and line up. I gots de love of Jesus in dese tits."

Preacher Hardin say, "Julie Ola Faye, the love of Jesus is not limited nor or his ways."

Masta Johnny right. Some men de Laud chooses to bring into de kingdom while dey lie down at a womans side nursin de sweet love of Jesus from de tit.

"Jest have em line up, Sheriff. Dere is nuff love for all. Dis ole mule wont mind. He jest eatin de corn and de blood and dis ole upside down hog dont mind. He jest watch and bleed and watch and bleed."

Yes, laudy, and den dat ole white bear hound come and sits on all de mens and eats out dey throats so dey cans go straight up to Jesus dat loves em jest like Wesley loves em wid his gun. Jest sending all dem mens up to Jesus. Wesley loves in his special way and you mens knows he loves you. You can feels it in yo gut when he loves you and when Jimmy boy loves you too like Wesley teach em. Jest loves yo mens right up to Jesus.

Oh dat Jimmy boy, slippin out of de house at night when dey is all sleep and comin down here to talk his heart out to his ole nigger mammy and doin hit since he twelve and his mama and papa die. Jest comin in to his Mama Julie and talkin out his heart.

Blessin on you, you ole nigger mammy, lovin on dat Jimmy boy. But Jesus jest such a boy. I woulda loved on dat boy Jesus too. Den he wouldnt die of a broken heart de way he did. But dat Jimmy boy caint do it no more cause his ole nigger mammy gonna die.

Masta Hardin say, "Julie Ola Faye, Jesus works in many ways his wonders to perform."

One night I dreams dat all de Mockinbirds in de world was hollerin at de same time and all de cows was bawlin and all de mules brayin and all de babies cryin. Nothin wouldnt be quiet no where. I thought I gonna go crazy. I trys to hide in de trees and hide in de dirt but dat dont do no good. I runs off to de mountains and den I wents down under de water but de mountains was cryin and de water was cryin and de dirt and de trees was cryin and den I was shoutin and cryin too. I trys to stop but I couldn't stop and den all of a sudden hit was so still and so quiet I hears a feather float down breakin through de air as hit fell and when dat feather hit de ground a voice cry out from de heavens *"Behold, John Wesley Hardin is dead. Now men everywhere can walk in peace for he who sought their lives is no more."*

"Now git out, mule. Go to de pasture. I gots to cut open dis hog belly for de chitlens and take out dese guts and throw em in de washin pan."

Oh, laudy, dey is comin for sho. I can sees em and hears em. Poor Julie Ola Faye. Pray to god, you nigger whore. If he would jest give me time, I could save de world wid love. I got enough for everybody. For mens and women and children. I would gather em into dese great busoms until dey gets quiet and lay down all their guns. Yes, Laud, I could. Yes. Jest say you *yes* to my *yes* and together we can save de world. Even so, Lord Jesus, come quick.

"What you mens want here? Whats you mean ridin in here wid all dat dust where a body caint pull her dress off to git cool while she kills her hog? Sheriff, caint you see I gots no clothes on! Whats you mens doin out here noway? Whos you lookin for?"

"Damn, Sheriff! Would you look at that. I aint never seen nothing like that before. Damn! I have heard about them tits, but I didn't believe it. No wonder John Wesley was—damn, man, would you look at that!"

"We have come after John Wesley, Mama Julie," the sheriff say.

"He aint here, Sheriff. I aint seen him neither. You mens better git on off now!"

Oh laudy, dey aint gonna go. Dey is gonna stay. Dey is gonna git down. Oh laudy, you ole nigger whore!

"Aint nobody knows de trouble I've seen. Aint nobody knows but Jesus. Oh laud, I'm gonna lay down my sword and shield down by de river side, down by de river side—oh laudy, sweet Jesus—"

"Come over here, Mr. Sheriff. I gots somethin for you here inside dis ole hog. Jest come over here closer to dis ole upside down hog."

Jim Stephens

After delivering the cattle to the railhead northeast of De Leon as promised and on schedule, Wes and I paid off our hands, and then Wes suggested we go on west a little space. We had not seen that part of Texas before, our previous wanderings being confined to the northern and eastern portions of the state. Since we had some twenty days before we needed to be back in Comanche for the races, we took our time and saw what we wanted to see as far as the more interesting parts of the country were concerned. Frequently, we would go miles out of the way to slake our curiosity about some physical protuberance upon the otherwise nearly flat and treeless prairie. Riding on some days no more than five miles and on others at least fifty, by the fifteenth of the month we had reached the famous Staked Plains of Texas.

Here, we turned more west, following one of the numerous forks of the Brazos River for some time until we ventured off to explore the upper reaches of the Yellowhouse Canyon along some thirty miles of its length, riding almost to its source before turning back north again. After about seventy-five miles of such meandering, we hit the famous Palo Duro stretch of the Prairie Dog Town Fork of the Red River, lying just east of the present town of Canyon. It was into this same general area a few months later that Colonel Ranald Mackenzie was to pursue the last remaining, sizeable band of Comanche Indians under Chief Quanah Parker.

In a famous battle in which the lives of a few Indians and several hundred horses and mules were lost, Mackenzie and his men effectively ended for all time the armed resistance of that famous and colorful people. Many, even to this day, would feel those adjectives not only too generous but in some instances outright lies, preferring "treacherous" and "murderous" in their places. Perhaps I would feel that way too, but then no Comanches ever killed my father and brothers, burned my home, or raped and murdered my mother or carried my sisters into bondage.

Curiously, in the short time the Hardins had lived in Comanche, the people of that town and county had gone to considerable lengths in relating to them numerous atrocities reputedly committed by these same famous and colorful people, with some of these deeds occurring less than five years before the Hardins' arrival. But to have traveled through the county on horseback in the year of 1874 and to have seen the several small settlements and the many prosperous farms, you would have sworn there had never been an Indian in those parts. It just goes to show how quickly the Texas frontier was changing in those days, and as I consider those times again, I see they clearly foreshadowed the demise of Wes and his type, though neither of us recognized it back then. However popular and illustrious that type was, the kind of life Wes led was beginning to die out by the middle seventies, though in far West Texas it did last a few years longer.

Upon reaching the site of present-day Amarillo, we laid in fresh provisions and there turned southwest, intending to follow the Terra Blanco Creek on west out of Texas. We spent that night with a small band of Comanches camped around a big spring on what is now called Palo Duro Creek. While there we made the acquaintance of a young breed Indian called Charlie Buffalo and his Comanchero father. Upon their advice we turned back north until we encountered the Canadian River and from there back west up the Canadian River Valley toward the New Mexico territory. All in all, we had been traveling steadily for ten days, not to mention the larger part of some nights. During that time and along the five hundred miles we covered, we rode through or close by many small communities that had established themselves around springs or along trade routes in the wake of several years of cattle drives to Kansas and points farther north. The great Buffalo hunts that were just beginning in that area encouraged settlement, also. Of course, many of the communities had no names at the time we saw them, but later they became the thriving and prosperous towns of Albany, Abilene, Stamford, Sweetwater, Snyder, Post, Lubbock, Canyon, and Amarillo, to name only a few.

When finally Wes and I stopped our trek west, we were within a few miles of the New Mexico border. Instead of going on, however, we turned aside to spend a couple of days at a small settlement on the Canadian River known as Tascosa. Had it not been for the races back in Comanche, we might have pushed on west to Santa Fe, and might have done so even at that, trusting Wes's brother Joe to run our horses for us, except Wes wanted to place his own bets as he felt he had a sure winner in the horse Rondo. In point of fact, our latest cattle drive had not been profitable and we were short of cash. Also, our troubles in Gonzales had deprived Wes of his usual gambling successes. We had been broke before and expected to be again, but Wes's roll as husband had increased his responsibility and added an urgency to our actions that not only kept our trip west from being as enjoyable as it might have been but overshadowed other considerations as well. Wes was also troubled by his upcoming birthday. He would be twenty-one and was concerned that he was not settled into some kind of profession as were his father and brother. I felt a similar uneasiness, though of a different nature. I chafed under the need to be on my own as well as to be working at something I would not feel the need to apologize for.

At any rate, after spending a couple of days and nights at Tascosa, in which time Wes made many new acquaintances, some almost as widely known and as notorious as he, we started back. Riding continuously, though not hard, we reached the Hardin farm by the 24th of May. This gave Wes time to ride each of the horses that would be racing until they were thoroughly winded and then let them rest up for a day before we put them in the race on Saturday and placed our bets.

All in all, the excursion Wes and I took into West Texas had not been unpleasant. I saw miles of new country, some of which I liked as well as any country I have seen, and I met new people with new ideas. Looking back, I understand those ideas shaped the state in the remaining years before the turn of the century just as surely as the reigning ideas that were responsible for Wes and his violence shaped the years after the war.

Despite the impression I may give from time to time, I do not regret the years I spent with Wes, though such a sentiment must be foreign to most people. I have always wondered what would have been the response of those cultured gentlemen on the train that day riding southwest out of Chicago had I told them of my life with John Wesley Hardin—surprise at the least, even a little of shock perhaps, but more than likely a considerable disbelief and incredulity, thinking me at the least to be a spinner of tall tales and at heart an habitual liar and a fraud. It was for those reasons, except in the most guarded circumstances, that I always refrained from acknowledging I knew Wes. Such seemed the best practice and a matter of good sense.

The 26th of May 1874 saw a large crowd at the track, horse racing and the subsequent gambling that went with it being popular in the Comanche area during those years as well as in most parts of Texas. Besides, for several weeks news of the races had been published in the county and in the surrounding counties as well. Another reason for the intense interest was that horses had value beyond what they would bring at sale. An individual was known by the horseflesh he rode, and for a man to have the best horse that cash and ingenuity could secure was a matter of deepest pride. In truth, a man's horse was as important in his eyes and in those of the community at large as his profession or his skill with a gun. Such an explanation might seem redundant, yet much of the glamour and romance that once surrounded the horse has faded, despite its continued importance as transportation. Indeed, I find it hard to believe such times existed at all. It's amazing how severely twenty years alter a man's thinking as well as his values.

In this, I am not trying to be philosophical but am only pointing out how the major social event—and major social event it indeed was, with full dress and finery and visiting kinfolks—got to be the major social event. Not even hangings were more popular. Given the large numbers of people in attendance that day at Comanche Track, it was easy for Wes to place several advantageous bets. The Hardin family was relatively unknown in this part of the state, except for Wes, and even here Wes's reputation lay in another area than gambling, with the result that many people bet with him quite readily just for the privilege of being able later to tell their families and friends they had bet on a horse race with the infamous John Wesley Hardin, notorious outlaw and killer to date of at least forty men. Whether they won was of little or no importance. The mere touch of celebrated flesh occasioned by the simple passing of money from one hand to the other was their object and ample compensation for any loss, be it ready cash or a prized horse and saddle. In addition to the bets Wes placed, a number of others were made by his friends, including myself and Joe Taylor, and by Wes's brother Joe, who was beginning to build a reputation as a lawyer in town and for whom the added distinction of knowing horses could only aid his success in his profession.

As you might suspect, the races in Comanche that day turned out as we had known they would. Rondo ran first and won easily. Shiloh came next and had a walk over. Then came Dock in something of a closer race but which he still won by a good six feet. The only surprise was that Mavis Ansley and his father came in to the races and after a slight deliberation bet heavily against Rondo, the horse that Wes had purchased from them and which they had raised. I overheard old man

Ansley tell a number of people that the horse would not run and if it did that it was too slight to hold up over the distance. Standing there listening to him talk, I must admit I had my doubts about having put big money on a horse that had never run in a race and was relatively untested. I should have known better, of course. Wes was too good a judge of horseflesh not to recognize when his opponent had a winning entry or to run an animal of his own that was not clearly superior.

In all, Wes won over $3000 in cash that day, in addition to fifty head of cattle, two wagons, and fifteen saddle horses, which upon receipt he loaned to their previous owners until they could procure other mounts. In spite of this good fortune at the expense of others, the crowd bore Wes no ill feeling. Indeed, the same people who had lost their money to him, crowded around after the races offering to buy him drinks at the saloons in town later in the day. In deference to good will, Wes accepted many of these magnanimous offers. Such response to Wes surprised no one as he was a hero to many people in Texas despite his reputation as a killer. Only those ignorant of his ways or those jealous of his success ever wished him any harm. I suspect it was this last which brought old John Selman to shoot him in the back in El Paso. I know it wasn't courage or regard for the law, or even the well being of the good folk of Acme Saloon.

Anonymous

Still furiously beating the gangling
white mule across its ample rump with the flat of the shotgun
barrels, the Reverend Hardin had leaned forward until his
head was vertically aligned with that of the mule as if the one
second sooner such a posture might speed his arrival would
be vitally important to the success of his mission. With his
eyes preened straight ahead and bulging a little as though he
might be trying to see not only across distance but through
time as well, he saw first the angled, cornered, false-fronted
tops of the buildings beginning to emerge out of the natural
obscurity of the live oak grove in the middle of which the town
of Comanche had been built.

Not unlike last year's corn in an early summer pea patch,
the town had sprouted up amid the live oaks, volunteer and
sporadic, taking its beams and floors and walls and rafters
and shingles and finally board sidewalks from the trees felled
to create the square. Without plan, the small shotgun shops
and one night hotels and saloons were set in a soft circle
around a confusion of cattle pens and hitching rails. Just off
the square to the east sat a single small building which served
as a temporary courthouse, housing the sheriff's office and
jail in a single room up front and the judge's chambers and
his courtroom in the back—a building whose replacement only
a couple of years later would be more than ten times that
size, although containing still principally the sheriff's office,
the jail and the judge's chambers and courtroom. Outside the

cattle pens and hitching rails would be gone for the most part and grass planted from the stone sidewalks in to the foundations of what people now proudly called *The Courthouse.* An even more magnificent, native stone courthouse would be built some years later, as well as a new jail, but by then the town would sport its own railroad and a new gin and a mill for oil and have every intention of becoming a city—a city which would not want the notoriety of its small town past. Moving the jail around the corner and out of sight would be one step in that direction.

These forces for change, already in the air in the mid 70s, brought the Comanche of the 1900s into being. As surely as did the lawlessness by which he lived, they also brought the Reverend Hardin's son John Wesley to his appointed end. Even by the 1890s the small shotgun shops and saloons and one night hotels would be largely gone, and the blacksmith shop become also a livery. Likewise, the trading post would give way to large mercantile businesses such as Higginbotham & Company with their names painted in square, white letters a yard tall along the front and sides of the building. In the case of Higginbothams, branch stores could be found in a dozen other towns of similar size scattered over central and West Texas. At any time of the day, freight wagons might be seen in front of these stores, piled high with straight-backed cane chairs and iron bedsteads and cotton mattresses and plain oak furniture come in on the train all the way from Austin. Of course, the town would have a new bank by the century's end as well, a taller and larger and more ornate structure, built not of wood but of rock and marble and iron with a new safe specially ordered from England—a safe so heavy it took twenty-five men and a dozen mules to set it in place and so large it could in turn hold the twenty-five men. In short, it was progress and respectability that brought John Wesley to his finish, years before old John Selman ended his life in the Acme Saloon in El Paso.

But it was the old Comanche the Reverend Hardin saw from the back of his galloping mule, though mostly just one of its buildings, glimpsed through the narrow tunnel down which he hurtled on the back of the white mule—the destroyed blacksmith shop.

A blacksmith shop and only a blacksmith shop, he thought. *Why, I would have figured a Hardin, any Hardin, would have been worth more than a blacksmith shop. Why at least a hotel or the bank, and John Wesley—why John Wesley should have been worth one whole side of the street. I guess forty men sent to their maker and that last one on your twenty-first birthday ain't the deed I once thought it to be. In fact, I guess it ain't even the killing that's important any more. If you really want to stir people up and get them all hot to hang you and burn a whole street full of buildings in your honor, then you have also got to rob their banks and their stage coaches and their trains, as well as kill one or two of them. But just simple killing— why it ain't hardly enough in these advanced times.*

As soon as the Reverend saw the smoking ruin, he knew the mob had burned the building out of frustration and anger and afterward stood by while it burned, refusing to let anyone near the fire to put it out. Then he was close enough to smell the horse and mule flesh which had perished along with the building.

God damn you! he thought. *God Damn you whoresome bastards, you!*

Unconsciously, even as the shotgun was waving at the end of his outstretched arm, the Reverend pulled back the hammers and set them, and without breaking stride came on. Though the town loomed around him now, his mind's eye was fixed still upon the one object he had seen in the air above his head riding the long, slow furious miles into town—not the buildings nor the smoking blacksmith shop nor even the grove itself as if in the sheer spectacle of violence that had occurred there had vanished altogether, but the single large live oak in the square and from it suspended the dangling body of his son. Almost from the time he mounted the mule back in the field, he had berated himself. *Why didn't you start as soon as you saw the smoke?* he had thought, over and over again. *Why didn't you? When you first saw it, maybe then he still had a gun and a handful of shells to go in it and so could have lasted until you got there. So why didn't you! Why did you have to wait for somebody to ride all the way out there and on top of that waste precious seconds explaining what you had already guessed? Why did you! A man who does that to his sons don't deserve to have any, and now maybe you have got one less and maybe five minutes from now you will be dead yourself. What has killed a John Wesley Hardin won't hesitate to start in on its father, shotgun or not. Since you didn't start as soon as you saw the smoke, you might as well have stayed where you were until they remembered he even had a father and so came out there after you. That way they would at least have had to work to get you. So why didn't you start sooner? Why in thunderation did you wait!*

And so the Reverend came on, riding that last hundred yards on the white mule as furiously as he had ridden the four miles, with the shotgun waving in a circle over his head like the great and vengeful sword of the Lord, which he now believed it was. Another hundred yards behind him came the single rider pushing the winded, lathered race horse for all it was worth just to stay in sight, and still another hundred behind that the great white bear of a dog, tongue out, loping like the horse.

Hearing his support behind him, or believing he could, the Reverend still envisioned himself as leading a host of archangels that numbered in the hundreds of thousands, and stretched out beyond these like a great sea rolled a massy army dressed in gold and carrying swords of the finest steel. The din of its approach was like distant thunder, and before it the earth trembled in awe—an army of saints assembled in the name of the most high God and come to bring mercy to the oppressed and justice to the wronged and judgement and wrath to the damned, among whom would surely be those who had maligned and finally killed his son.

A mighty host of warriors representing God almighty, and he, the Reverend J. G. Hardin, their leader—but for thirty years he had fought alone. He had fought in every county in every state from Missouri to Texas and to a lesser degree in states both east and north of those, carrying in his hand the weapon of the holy word and crying out as he fought the eternal love of Jesus; for thirty years from one two-bit backwater town to another on the back of a horse spreading the gospel of redemption, and now it had come to this. The Lord of Hosts had heard his prayer in the wilderness and his cry of frustration in the hour of need, but despite his faith in the deliverance of the just, among whom he counted himself and his son, he could not help thinking, *What if they have hanged my son already? What if? God parted the waters of the Red Sea, and He stopped the sun from going around the earth, and He raised Lazarus from the dead, and then, in the form of his son, He came alone and unaided out of the black closed tomb of his own death. Thus what is one more body to be restored to breath? So what if they have? Is a broken neck and a half dozen bullet holes more difficult than six hours on a cross and three days in a tomb? Huh? Is it? So what if?*

And still the Reverend came on, riding furiously, hell bent, not seeing the buildings in whose shadows he now rode, but beyond them to the tree in the square, depending on the mule to thread his narrow way between the buildings without killing them both before he got a chance to use the shotgun, and still thinking, *You have still got to hurry, but whether you are in time or not, it will be necessary later to pull up your family and move on. Because you were wrong. This is obviously not the one spot in all the earth that God has Picked! Chosen! Set Aside! No, He wants you to build yet one more house and dig yet one more well. Yes, now I know that it is not the promised land and that I must leave. And leave I full well intend to do—that is if God will only spare my son that I may move out of this Christ-forsaken land with everything I moved into it with and with the same balance between what is not breathing and what is, but if He will not permit it, if He has allowed that lawless, degenerate mob of drifters and Sunday Christians and stinking buffalo hunters and crooked Texas Rangers to*

*hang him, then I don't care what I just said. I'll be damned if
I'll move even one more mile! Even one more inch! And though
He kill my horses and my mules and my hogs where they graze
in the pasture and my dog where it sleeps under the porch and
destroy my cotton in the fields and my remaining children in
their beds and then smite my person with sores and boils from
the crown of my head to the sole of my foot, still I will not move
even one more mile! One more inch! Do you hear my words,
Lord? I won't do it! I swear I won't do it! Nor will I ever again
preach the gospel. I swear I will lay down that book and I will
never pick it up again except to point out to everyone I meet
that it is a damn lie out of the mouth of a damn liar and that
there is no fear nor respect to be found in it, but only weakness,
and no kindness nor love, but only selfishness. And finally I
will tell them there is no God and there never has been, but
only the same dry barren leaves of loneliness and self pity blown
by the puny imagination of man through his own sick mind
for tens of thousands of years! I swear I will!*

Above the Reverend in the air as he came on, the old buried
violence raced too, and the old dead past from a time five years
before swirled just above his head and from five years before
that, and on back until it was no longer his own savagery and
anger and destruction he rode through but that of all men
everywhere and for all time who had ever been wronged and
sought to repay the wrong in turn. Clearly he saw these
wronged, their eyes flashing with both grief and lust, their
hands trembling with the need to shed blood and to kill, and
in their minds that awful loneliness and despair with which
he had just addressed the Lord. Indeed, he saw it all as he
had seen it before, including also the damned with their
phantom steeds, dead eyed and foam streaked, thundering in
his head, breathing fire and blood with their grim-lipped
masters mounted on their backs, the gaunt, thin-lipped
specters eternally cursing God and crying out as they rode,
Death! Death! Death! He saw their outstretched arms waving
wildly in front of them and their broad, quick swords streaked
with the blood of widows and orphans and martyrs and wives,

Christian and Pagan alike. He saw also all bravery and courage and truth and love and compassion and decency crouched and quivering before them. And then finally between two of the buildings he saw the top of the oak in the square but not yet what hung from its branches.

His response to God—that much the Reverend Hardin was certain of, or thought he was. As for the rest he could not say. What he might do if his son were already dead when he reached the square, he was unsure about also. In moments of rationality, he saw he could not defend himself against the mob. He could never hope to kill them all or even a few of them. That of course was not his intention, and it had never been. It was his own failure of forethought, of logic and reason, that he was angry about—and that not so much because he had not come sooner but that he had even considered for a moment that he could help John Wesley. It was not that one more gun would not have helped, but that it would have helped only for the moment and only in this instance. This was today, but there was always tomorrow and the day after that, and he could not spend every day for the remainder of his life with a loaded gun in his hand and a saddled horse standing at the ready. He was too old for that.

By now the Reverend's pace had slowed perceptibly, although the square and the more open view it afforded were still a dozen yards away. He did not know what he expected to find when he came into the open, but he did know he had to slow down to gain control over the shotgun, which he fully expected to have to use, if only in his own defence. Though the pause had been slight, it was sufficient that the rider following him was now within shouting range.

"Wait, Hardin!" the man cried with the little strength he had left. "Wait, damn you! There is something you don't know—something I forgot to tell you. Wait, Hardin!"

Then his voice gave out, and he settled back into the frustration he had felt when he first saw the fresh mule begin to put distance between Hardin and himself and the worn out horse he rode, thinking all the way into town, You are one

damned fine race horse! I know. I have seen you run. I have
even put money down on you and not been sorry afterward
that I did it. But I hope somebody knocks me down if I ever do
it again, because when it really counts you ain't no damned
good at all! If you belonged to me, I would shoot you as soon
as you stop, just out of principle. I swear I would. Now the
only hope I've got of stopping that crazy preacher is his flat-
faced, cross-eyed mule. Maybe that mule ain't never been that
close to a building before, much less two of them, and likely
as not stands as good a chance of running slapdab into one or
the other of them as he is of making it through unscathed and
so knock Hardin off onto the ground and if luck continues
break his leg.

  If the Reverend heard the man's cry, he gave no sign, and
as he threaded his way between two of the tall wooden
buildings that offered the only entrance into the square from
that direction, he was still thinking, *Whether coming shielded
in the righteousness and wrath of the Lord or just in personal
anger and indignation, they will be expecting me. They would
have to be. What father would do less? It is the more I might
do they will be unsure about, and there I may possibly have
the advantage. Perhaps they will be expecting the grief of what
I see to incapacitate me, but in that I will have them fooled.
After six years, nothing that he does or that happens to him
can come as a surprise. When you have lived for six years
expecting to suffer grief, how devastating can the grief be once
it comes? So I will be the one with the advantage of surprise.
The first blast of this shotgun will give me that and quite
possibly the advantage of grief too, if any one of them is close
enough to take the full charge. The second barrel should carry
me into their middle and give me time to reload once. Like I
say, I may not be able to save him. The gap between feeling
and action may be farther than the distance between my farm
and this damn town. It may be as long as years, and there is
no way I could make that up in just one four-mile ride on the
back of a mule. Hell, I don't know what it would have taken to
forestall this end. What I do know is that once a long time ago,*

I took a son up on a mountain and stripped him bare and prepared to slay him with my knife and would have, but a voice stayed my hand, saying, "You can. You even will. That is enough. That is all that is required of you." Then I said to my son, "Rise up, your time is not yet come." And it was all right for me to do it because I am a Father, but it is not all right for them to do it. And once a long long long time ago, I even stood by while another mob took a son of mine and brought him to trial and found him guilty and then went out and hanged him spread eagled on a crossed tree, and I just stood by, because I had something to prove. For six hours I let him hang there and for three days I let him lie inside the grave until the smell of his rot was sour in my nostrils. Then it was enough, and I went out and got him and brought him home. But I'll be damned if there is anything left to prove, and maybe I am a little late because the action should have proceeded the feeling, but I will not stand by and see it happen a second time. By God in heaven I will not!

And so oblivious to all danger, or at least to all caution, the Reverend Hardin rounded the corner by the bank, seeing the last obstacle fall away to reveal, not the hanging body of his son, John Wesley, but the crowd he expected beneath the oak and seven ropes he could count dangling from the limbs, all of them so new the curl had not yet fallen out. His first thought was that the mob intended to use five of the ropes to hang John Wesley, Jimmy Boy, Joe, Jeff and himself, and the other two on the women. But even as he thought it—and as if by reflex, since as soon as it happened he could not remember doing it—his finger closed on the trigger of the shotgun. He did not even know what he had done until he saw the leaves on the oak come loose and begin to rain down in pieces on the milling crowd. Then for the first time he heard the sound go off in his ear and felt himself rock gently back on the mule.

Only then did the Reverend realize that he was shouting at the crowd, and had been even before he fired the shotgun. What he said was uncertain—something about angels and God and the sword of divine vengeance and justice—but to his mind it was the most eloquent and powerful utterance he had ever heard. Then suddenly he knew that he had heard it one other time and one time only. The world had heard it too and also only one time. Once again he saw the bright darkness on top of the high desert mountain and heard about him the black thunder and watched the finger of pure fire write the law into the stone and listened in awe and terror to the voice of Jehovah. Whether it had come out of his mouth this second time he couldn't tell. It was inside him like a great voice yet it was around him in the air, somehow both beyond him and above him, and he found himself trembling before its force along with the crowd.

The crowd, by the way, stood in abject amazement, their guns still unraised, the surprise of his terrible coming affecting them as he had surmised it would. Actually, they were caught up in the wonder of being fired upon by a solitary maniac riding a snow white mule and shouting scripture at the top of his voice and could only guess what motive or hope of success lay behind his insane action.

As for the Reverend Hardin, he was absolutely sure God had spoken through him, announcing the terrible and eminent destruction of an unloving and unfaithful people; and hearing behind him now the sounds of the man on his exhausted horse and the bear hound's thudding lope, he thought, not "my friend and my dog," but "the archangels of the most high, ranked and arrayed for battle, their shields bossed and shining in the sun, their wings beating luminous, heavy and powerful, and their swords striking sparks of bright lightning in the cool evening air."

"Hallelujah! Hallelujah!"

Jim Stephens

All in all Wes and I had a fine and exciting time at the track the morning of his birthday. The remainder of the day, filled as it was likely to be with celebration including good food and drink and gambling as well, promised more of the same. The only negative thought we entertained was that having established a reputation in the county as proven winners where horse racing was concerned, we would never again be able to do as well with our betting. Such an outcome, however, mattered little at the time. We were among friends and had just won a great deal of money, which would keep us both up for some time to come as well as allow Wes to provide for his wife and to a degree the rest of his family as well.

Surprisingly enough, some of the money was earmarked for the expansion of the farm. Although he had entertained the notion for years, Wes was now serious about going into the farming business with his father, a joint venture from which they both expected to profit handsomely. I was, of course, invited to join in, and quite frankly I looked forward to a more settled life, though I would not have admitted it at the time. Despite the romance and intrigue our solitary fugitive existence provided, I was tired of being on the run. What is more, although I had known my father for only a few years and my mother almost not at all, the influence of their ideas and way of life upon me had given me a foundation in decency. I knew if they were still alive they would strongly disapprove of my association with Wes and would be ashamed of the escapades I had been involved in. I believe this influence more than any other responsible for the growing discontent I felt with myself and what I was doing with my life. Still, I was satisfied for the moment and saw no obstacles ahead that Wes and I couldn't handle. Or so it seemed at the time, but then neither Wes nor I had figured on Charley Webb. Indeed, no thought of him had crossed our minds since the night at Mrs. Waldrups.

That day at the races in Comanche changed everything for Wes. I am persuaded that from that moment on until the end of his life, a morning did not dawn that was free of thoughts of Charley Webb. However remorseful those thoughts and tinged with regret, Wes had to feel a certain satisfaction in the fact that although he had gone to prison Webb had lost his life. Still, many a night, lying sleepless in his cell, he must have wished he had taken another course of action. But had he done so, he would not have been John Wesley. And if by some fate Webb had not been shot that day, sooner or later in some other place it would have been someone like Webb. But fate is fate, and however unfortunate for Wes, Webb's foolhardy act worked to my favor. Had I not gotten out when I did, my chances of living even to twenty-one would have been slender.

As I have said, Wes and I had forgotten about Charley Webb, but almost from the time we arrived at the track and were recognized until we walked into Jack Wright's saloon a couple of hours later, we had to listen to people talk about the deputy sheriff of Brown County. It seems everyone present knew his name and had some knowledge of his intentions, although few had ever seen him and no one we talked to knew him personally. As it turned out, Webb had made threatening remarks about Wes on several occasions. No one seemed to know exactly what he had said, though each man had his opinion. Generally, their comments echoed Webb's belief that Wes and his band of cut-throat murderers—meaning me among others, I presume—would never be content to live in Comanche and confine their activities to that county alone but would eventually frequent neighboring Brown County as well. To forestall that end, Charley Webb intended either to capture Wes Hardin or kill him, thus putting a finish once for all to that noted public menace. It was said he had entered Comanche County that same day at the head of fifteen armed men for the express purpose of confronting Hardin and his gang at the race track and there to shoot it out.

As soon as Wes and I heard these stories, we put them down as exaggerated. We had heard similar ones in the past. Men drink, and in resulting moments of deranged judgement make boasts and claims which they otherwise would not make and which even in their drunkenness they have no intention of standing behind. Neither their pride nor their acquaintances require it of them. This is the way the game is played, and most understand the rules and abide by them.

While some of the stories we heard had more substance than others, all but a couple proved unfounded. One tale in particular had it that Webb had met Wes a number of times and backed him down, in each case sparing his life while giving him a warning to leave Texas and never return. Hearing this, one would believe Webb possessed of great magnanimity as well as great courage. Had I not known Wes, this account might have impressed me also, but the tale does not go on to explain why after repeated humiliating encounters with his amiable persecutor, resulting in loss of pride and reputation, Wes still insisted on inhabiting the same part of Texas as Webb. It also does not explain why every other man in both Brown and Comanche Counties still feared and respected Wes, though this particular one did not.

After talking among ourselves, Wes, Jim Taylor, and I decided that Webb was likely the instigator of most if not all of the tales, though a certain truth requiring caution on our part ran through them all, that being Webb's obvious desire to be the man who would one day kill John Wesley Hardin. This intention made Webb a dangerous man, no matter his character otherwise, but our acknowledgement of that fact did little to dampen our spirits. After all, no one we talked to had seen Webb that day, but what if they had? It would have been insane for a man, despite his bravery and skill with a gun, to confront Wes with so many of his friends present. Even to challenge Wes alone would have been foolish. He was too good, too fast, too sure of himself. That's what made him Wes Hardin. I saw a number of top gun hands over the years, a few of them so superior to the average gun hand that they were famous, but I never met a man I believed to be Wes's equal.

Among the many exaggerated accounts of Webb's words and behavior we were treated to that morning, two were of substance, as I have noted. In both cases we knew the men who related the stories and had no reason to doubt their accounts. One said he had heard Webb call John Carnes, the sheriff of Comanche, a dirty low down scoundrel and a coward because he allowed John Wesley and his band of murderers to stay in town. Webb had gone on to say that Carnes was no sheriff at all and should not be allowed to call himself that and furthermore should resign and leave the county since he was the reason the county had no real protection against the lawless. Now we knew John Carnes personally. He was a friend of ours and certainly no coward. For Webb to say this about him suggested he had little regard for anyone except himself. Either that or he was a damn fool.

The other story which we believed to be true was also told to us by a man who was present when it happened and whom we knew to be as trustworthy as the first. It seems that a few days before the races Webb had arrested an entire cow camp a short distance from Comanche and had singled out a particular man, insisting that he was John Wesley Hardin, although the man denied it as did his associates. Webb then proceeded to berate the man, telling him he was afraid of his own name and jabbing him in the side with a gun. Before he left, he made the man get down on his knees and beg for his life. Though Webb knew for a fact that Wes was not in the county at the time, he humiliated this man in front of his friends just for the purpose of building up his reputation. The man who gave us this information went on to verify Webb's knowledge of Wes's absence from the county by relating an earlier encounter between Webb and one of his deputies in which Webb had been plainly told of our trip to the Panhandle of the state. This incident showed Webb to be a fraud and a loud-mouthed bully.

Because of these cowardly actions, Webb did not seem a serious threat. By mid-morning, Wes had started to make fun of him, saying he hoped Webb would leave off killing him until dark or perhaps altogether. As for me, it was beginning to look like the Jack Helms incident all over again, except Helms had not been a coward. Webb seemed to be that and much more, and thus not someone we needed to fear, that is as long as we had friends willing to watch our backs.

And so for the second time we put Webb out of our minds, and if we had not been able to do that on our own, the excitement of the races would have done it for us. The fascination of watching the horses run and the equally keen anticipation of our winnings were simply too great.

After the races, Wes and I and some of our friends went immediately into town to celebrate our success at the track. With us was a small group of local men, including some of the well known citizens of the town, who respected Wes as a man even more than they respected his abilities with a gun. After taking a leisurely afternoon meal at a boarding house off the square, we were all going from bar to bar, drinking a little and joking around, but mostly Wes and I were trying to spend foolishly a little of the money we had won.

Though Wes never drank heavily, the few drinks he had that afternoon affected his behavior. In one saloon he threw a handful of twenty dollar gold pieces down on the bar and ordered up drinks for everyone present. Of course, the bartender and a couple of Wes's friends gathered up the money and gave it back to him because they believed him too drunk to know what he was doing, but despite their alarm and concern he was not drunk. Knowing him as I did, I saw this as a familiar ploy he had adopted for his own protection. It placed those who might wish to take advantage of him through surprise a little off their guard by making them less cautious, while allowing Wes to be as alert and watchful as ever. Wes's friends didn't realize this, however, and began to caution him about his drinking, worried as they were of his ability to defend himself if he got into a fight. He listened to this advice and upon considering it decided to humor them. He sent his younger brother Jeff to the stable for a horse and buggy in which we would all ride out to his father's farm where Julie Ola Faye was preparing us a family supper. I noted that it seemed a suitable ending for a fine and successful day, and Wes said he thought so too. Just before leaving, he invited all present up to Jack Wright's Saloon where he intended that we would have a last drink and then get in the buggy and accompany his two brothers out to the farm where his parents and his wife were waiting.

When we reached Jack Wright's, Frank Wilson, a deputy under Carnes came up and took Wes aside, saying to him, "Wes, I want to see you."

Wilson was by reputation a fair man and well respected, so Wes said "All right, Frank."

We stepped outside into an alley behind the saloon to see what Frank had to say.

"John," he began, putting his hand on Wes's shoulder, "the people here have treated you well. Now don't drink anymore, but go home and avoid all trouble."

Again, Wes said all right, and after allowing Wilson to check his person for a pistol we walked back toward the saloon. Had Wilson been better acquainted with Wes, he would have known to check also inside his vest where he always carried a spare gun. Just as we started to walk back to the door of the saloon, Jim Taylor came up to us and said, "Wes, you have drunk enough. Let us go home. Here is Jeff with the buggy."

"Let us go in and get a cigar," Wes replied. "Then we will go home."

But at this point we both noticed a man, a stranger, walking down the alley toward us from the west and wearing two six shooters. About this time, Dave Carnes remarked, "Here comes that damned Brown County sheriff!"

Anonymous

But the voice of God or not and archangels or not or how many, by then the Reverend Hardin already had one leg swung off the back of the mule. Dismounting even as he rode, he felt the gun in his hand go off a second time and saw yet more leaves come to pieces on the tree and begin to fall. Beneath the tree, men were scurrying like the doomed rats he now believed them to be. It was as if they had taken the first shot to be an accident but now knew it to be a case of misjudgment and if they stood still any longer Mr. Hardin would surely kill them.

As yet the Reverend had not seen his son or any of his son's friends. So maybe I am still in time, he thought. Maybe they were going to play with him awhile and then kill him. Maybe they didn't count on this interlude at all and furthermore maybe they counted too much on the grief and the surprise, hoping that by seven o'clock they would have us both swinging and by seven-thirty the rest of us and so finish in time for supper.

The Reverend was off the white mule and running now, crouched low, moving east along the north side of the square. He was headed for the cover of a freight wagon still parked in front of the burning blacksmith shop, breaking the shotgun as he ran and putting in two fresh shells while his eyes searched widely for any sign of his son. He looked also for someone to shoot, expecting at the same time to be shot at, though he had decided riding in that a death by shooting was preferable to one by hanging. Unless something came up in his favor and damn quick, he felt he was done for. He had only six shells left with two of them already in the gun.

The Reverend had reached the wagon by now, and crouched behind one wheel he finally gave himself time to breathe, sliding down behind the huge wooden spokes that were as long as a man's arm and so thick and tough they might as well have been steel for all the regard they had for simple bullets. For a full ten seconds he did not move, and then getting up on one knee he looked once more for his son, more carefully this time. What he saw he saw as if in a dream with himself paralyzed and unable to do anything but watch in astonishment. It was as if half of him was angry and scared and screaming out, over and over, *Run! Hide! Shoot! Run! Shoot!* while the part of him that thought and reasoned had chosen to ignore it all, saying simply, Let it alone. It will pass. Just pretend it is some kind of traveling show and try to enjoy it. When you wake in the morning, you will feel a whole lot better and probably you won't even remember why you were so concerned.

For the first time since leaving the cotton patch, the Reverend Hardin recognized who it was that had followed him those four miles into town, and he understood now the gravity of the situation he had hurled himself into. The element of surprise had indeed been his. What is more, his sudden charge combined with the firing of the shotgun and his frenzied, half crazed shouting were likely the only reasons he was still alive. Obviously, the surprise had worn off. Shots seemed to be coming from all sides of the square, where men of one persuasion fired upon those of another. The Reverend could not make out who was who, but either way he knew neither side considered him a threat or had much respect for his shotgun. To them it might as well have been only a large stick with a longer reach than most sticks. He knew too that which ever side wanted to end his son's life still had that goal firmly in mind, intending finally to hang him up in the square by his neck even if he was already dead by then and could feel neither the pain of the rope nor the shame of it.

Coinciding with these brief moments of clear, reasoned thinking, the Reverend saw his friend round the same corner by the bank where he had entered the square and at a fast trot begin to cross the square toward where he huddled behind the wheel of the wagon. Seeing the danger his friend was in, the Reverend started to cry out, *Go back, Jake! Damn you, go back or they will kill you for sure! They don't care who they shoot, no matter that some of them are your friends. For God's sake, turn that worn out horse around and get out of town!*

The Reverend wanted to say it. He even tried to say it, but he couldn't. Something in his throat caught the words and held them so that only a strange, muffled cry such as a child might make came out. Then for a moment he was in the dream again, his reason gone, thinking, *See, I told you didn't have anything to worry about. Look at that old white mule. He is still standing in the very spot where you climbed off of him, caught exactly in the crossfire between those men under the tree and those in the saloon directly across from it with a hundred bullets been fired already. Not only has he not been hit, he hasn't even been disturbed enough to prevent him from going to sleep. Things don't have to make sense in dreams, so just sit back and enjoy it while it lasts, because it ain't real. In the morning you're going to remember all this and laugh about it.*

But even as the Reverend watched, the scene dim and opaque, the dream was fading. He saw the horse and rider frozen in their own slow furious motion and saw the horse stumble and begin to fall and heard the half dozen shots that must have killed it as soon as they hit it. One moment it was alive and running with everything left in it and the next it was dead and falling lifeless through the stilled space, its head only slightly bowed and its legs tucked under as though it might be jumping, only straight into the ground. Despite the horror, it was an action beautiful to see, beautiful and yet terrific, with the horse spiraling downward through the thick hot air yet moving almost not at all so that the Reverend could feel in his own body the strange, thick weightlessness, the slowed, strangled motion. Still high on his back, the rider followed the horse down, a curious look of peace on his face, blank of any worry or fear or even expectation of the dusty, thudding crash that was to come.

To the Reverend Hardin, horse and rider seemed to float down, to take whole minutes of time to move just inches toward the ground, and he thought first, *Good, the horse is dead. Maybe they will be satisfied with that. Maybe they were just angry they didn't get me, and now that they have killed the horse, they won't bother with Jake.*

Then in an instant, and still in the dream, the Reverend knew that Jake was dead, too. He had died along with the horse in the first volley of shots, and only the terrible lethargy of the fall suggested otherwise. In a final confused crumbling of legs and arms and heads, they fell, showering the dust for yards around with blood. *That was no dream!* the Reverend thought. *There was too much action and too much blood. I can taste the dust in my mouth and smell the blood. Dream, hell!*

Only then did the Reverend see the great dog, and back in the dream again, he watched it clear the square by the bank and come bounding across the open square, a large indistinct mass of brilliant white moving close to the ground and seeming not to run at all, but coming on at amazing speed. Then the men who had killed Jake and his horse saw it too. They walked now unprotected across the open square, advancing on the saloon where the Reverend suddenly realized his son must be. They had already formed into a line and started to walk when Jake charged into the square, and without so much as a pause they shot him down. Now they came on, ignoring the Reverend crouched behind the giant oak wheel of the freight wagon and ignoring the great white hound also. They considered the shotgun no threat, only a nuisance, and they must have felt the same way about the dog. Still, the dog came on, headed straight for the line.

For the first time since he left the cotton patch, the Reverend began to feel an emotion other than fear or anger.

Realizing what the dog's strength and bulk made him capable of, he silently cheered it on. *Kill the sons of bitches! he thought. Tear out their throats one by one until they break formation. Then I will cut the legs out from under them that are left so you can sit up on top of them while you chew.*

"Come on, Bear Boy, kill the sons of bitches!" he screamed.

Without bark or growl, the giant dog hit the end of the line, knocking the first two men sprawling into the dirt, their rifles falling and little short gasps of pain and disbelief escaping from their lips. From there, the dog went on to knock down three more men and send two others running for cover. Only then did the Reverend realize the dog was not on attack. He was trying simply to reach the wagon where the Reverend crouched behind the wheel and had taken the most direct route possible, but though he had almost made it, demobilizing half the line as he came, the Reverend saw he was unlikely to get much further. The men left standing were beginning to react.

"God damn cur!" one said, kicking the white mound of moving fur savagely in the side as it ran by.

"Damn son of a bitch!" another said, turning and intending to hit the dog with the barrel of his gun.

Up to now the men in the line must have seemed little more than large weeds to the dog, obstacles easier to run over than go around, but the kick changed his thinking. He gave a short yelp that turned into a growl, and almost in mid air he seemed to turn. He simply swung his hind quarters in the direction opposite of the kick and let the momentum carry his front half around. In a split second, lips tightened across clinched teeth, he was back on the man who kicked him, knocking him flat on his face and sinking his teeth into the man's shoulder, tearing loose a strip of skin and muscle.

"Oh hell!" the man gasped, instinctively throwing his hand over his face and expecting to feel the sharp white teeth at his throat. But the dog was no longer concerned with him. The man immediately beside him was bringing the club of his rifle around to his waist, meaning to blast the dog into hell if he could, but before he found the trigger with his finger he was on his stomach in the dirt, his rifle gone and forgotten. He had felt his jaw loosen and slide a little to one side as the dog hit him and now felt warm blood running out of his mouth where he had cut his tongue when he fell.

As incredible as it seemed to the Reverend, the whole episode from the time the dog entered the square until now had taken only seconds. Fully half the men were on the ground and the other half scrambling to give the dog room, where he was beginning to turn rapidly in ever widening circles, rushing any man who would not give ground. It was the most amazing display of strength and courage the Reverend Hardin had ever seen, as well as being unbelievable. In all the years he had owned the dog, he had never heard him growl. It was truly unbelievable, but it was also too good to last. Somewhere in the mill of men and dog, a shot rang out, slapping the dirt just inches from the dog's head. The Reverend saw how it had to end. Then he was back in the dream again, the shotgun heavy in his hands, the scene in front of him beginning to slow down and then to blur.

"Oh no!" he shouted. "No, damn it!"

The Reverend knew what he had to do, and at the same time, as in a dream, he was doing it—moving out from behind the wheel and beginning to run, bent low at the waist and firing the shotgun once, twice, BLAM! BLAM! as he ran. The expanding shot patterns caught the largest concentration of men in their upper bodies, and they begin to slap at themselves as if stung by bees. Now the Reverend was among them, holding the shotgun by the barrels and swinging it over his head like a club, knocking first one man senseless and then another. Turning his attention away from the dog and to its master, one of the few men still standing raised his shotgun and leveled it at the Reverend, but before he could fire the dog hit him full in the chest. By the soft limber windmilling of his arms and legs as he fell, the Reverend knew the dog had knocked the man senseless.

By now the Reverend Hardin had loaded the shotgun again, this time meaning to send a couple of the godless bastards still standing straight into hell, but the booming voice of John Carnes stopped that. Evidently the diversion created by the great white dog had given John Wesley time to clear the saloon as well as given the sheriff the opportunity he needed to gain control over the mob. While John Wesley and his friends made a run for their horses, the sheriff and his men took up positions in the street to prevent the reforming of the mob.

"I'll kill the first one of you that raises his gun!" the sheriff shouted out to the men surrounding the Reverend and the dog, and he was John Carnes and they knew he would. That's why they made him sheriff. Still, given the slightest chance, any one of them would have shot him dead, and he knew it.

"If I have to I'll kill the whole damn bunch of you!" he shouted again. And then one did raise his gun. He fired from the hip at the sheriff where he stood in the street, the bullet missing by inches and slamming into the wall behind him. Carnes shot him down before he could fire again, and then all hell broke loose. Men were running in every direction, shooting off their guns, the Reverend Hardin among them. With luck he made the front door of Jack Wright's Saloon, out of which his son had run only moments before. Once inside, he broke down the shotgun and stuffed in two fresh shells, already feeling easier now that he knew his son was still alive. *Now let the sons of bitches come!* he thought. *Now let them do what they will.*

Above him once more, the Reverend heard the clanging armor of the ranked archangels and the deadly rush of their swinging swords. Outside the sheriff had downed two more of the mob and brought the rest to surrender their arms, dropping them in the street and beginning to walk away. For a minute the Reverend had time to think again, and then out of the corner of his eye he saw the body of Charley Webb lying in the dirt along the wall of the saloon. It was sprawled face up in a pool of blood near the rear door, with the gaping hole in the center of the cheek, staring out like a third, off-center eye.

Then John Carnes was at the front door.

"You better get your mule and your dog and get out of here, Mr. Hardin. Maybe I can hold them until you get out of town, but I can't promise to protect you beyond that. Bill Waller and one group of men are already saddled and gone. You need to get home. I would go with you, but if I leave they will burn what is left of the town. You better go on. If you see John Wesley, you tell him I will let him know when it is safe to come back in and surrender himself."

"Thank you, John," the Reverend said. "God bless you! Come on, Bear. Let's go home."

Jim Stephens

It was too good to be true. It couldn't have lasted. I should have known that, and when I thought about it later I realized the only other fool in town that day besides Charley Webb was me. Of all the men present, I was the one who should have known better, even before Wes knew. Maybe I was never as accurate a judge of character as he was, but I knew all about percentages—arithmetic had been my best subject in school. But to what advantage? I might as well have gone out and bet all my money on the sun coming up in the west for the next five days in a row. It would have made as much sense. So when Dave Carnes said what he said, I came off with one of my own.

"Damn fool!" I said. "Damn empty headed fool!"

All present assumed I was talking about Charley Webb, as they were thinking the same thing themselves. One even said, "You are sho right about that, except you forgot to say, *That Damned Empty Headed Dead Fool!*"

But it wasn't Webb I was meaning. It was myself for thinking that Wes could go even one day without running into some kind of trouble. Wes Hardin and trouble were no wager that you bet on. It was more a kind of truth, an absolute, like putting a fully loaded gun to your head and pulling the trigger. Every man present knew that, and I should have too. I guess I wanted the other life Wes and I had talked about more than I realized, and that longing suspended my judgment.

But sure enough, when we took a good second look, the

man who resembled the description we had of Charley Webb was coming down the alley behind the saloon. He wasn't walking straight toward it exactly, more like he was sidling up to it, though it was definitely the saloon he was aiming for. It stuck me then he had to know we were in the alley, though he came on like someone who didn't have a care in the world. Had it not been for the pistols strapped around his waist and the fact that his eyes never for a moment shifted from our position, I would have sworn he was just out for a walk.

When Webb reached the end of the alley, he turned, and without breaking stride came on toward us. Only when he had advanced to within five steps of Wes did he stop. I don't know what Webb had on his mind. He didn't appear to have much of a plan. Maybe he just came out to look the place over and later on he intended on shooting Wes in the back. But he stood there so long staring at Wes I decided he was trying to convince himself there truly was a John Wesley Hardin and that the man he was looking at was the real McCoy. Finally, he turned and glanced around, giving the rest of us a clean look at his face. Only then did he open his mouth to speak, but Wes caught him off guard before he could say anything.

"Have you any papers for my arrest?" he asked.

A mock smile ran sideways across Wes's face, letting Webb know that if he didn't choose his words carefully, Wes full well intended to kill him. It was not the right comment for Wes to have made, and it bothered me more than I would have admitted. It was the same scene I had witnessed time and again, only played out in different towns before different audiences who had not seen it before. Suddenly, I didn't want to be a tough case anymore, a man feared just because I could handle a gun and had used it on occasion to shoot other men. Today especially I didn't want it. I was looking forward to a good meal at the Hardin farm and then a chance to light up a pipe and listen to old man Hardin talk about his crops and the government and the battles he might have fought in during the war if only his age and physical condition had not prevented him doing so.

Later, I wanted to go down to Julie Ola Faye's cabin for a while and let her tell me about her visions. I wanted to hear how God had appeared to her in a dream, telling her she was his prophet and then giving her a vision to prophesy about. Usually she would tell me about the one she had most often where the enemies of Wes would come rolling down on him in a thundering smoking wagon that moved forward without the aid of horses or mules. I was really looking forward to having a good time, but when Wes said what he did, I knew it wasn't going to happen.

As I have suggested, it was the same old Wes again, never openly provoking anything but then not saying the right words either—just half right, half wrong words so that if you were the man he was talking to, you could choose to let them go by or not, and if you did they were always words which allowed you to save face somewhat. Wes saw to that, but inside you knew you had backed down, and it was that which hurt and that you had to live with.

When he didn't get his answer from Webb right away, Wes repeated the question.

"I said, 'Do you have any papers for my arrest?'"

"I don't know you," Webb said.

It was a lie, and we all knew it was a lie, but just as John Wesley had suspected Webb had already decided for himself what honor was worth and what life was worth, and he had picked life as the better of the two. A lot of men I knew didn't have that much sense. Some didn't for sure. I was probably one of them and Wes was another.

"My name is John Wesley Hardin," Wes said, mocking Webb again, but Webb was prepared to back down all the way; and to be frank, I kind of admired him for doing it. Besides, he had come in from Brown County, and it was Brown County he had to go back to. He didn't have to prove anything in Comanche, and no matter what happened there he could always go back home and tell it differently.

"Now I know you," Webb said, "but I have no papers for your arrest."

It was the perfect answer as far as I could see. Here was a man who wanted to live above all else, as long as he could do it with a little pride. And I could understand what one of his reasons for wanting to live might be. Some months before the present trouble started, one of our friends had told Wes and me, "When you meet up with Webb you are going to be surprised because he is the most beautiful man you are ever likely to see."

Now I had seen him, and I knew that to be so. Still a young man, only twenty-six I was told later, Webb was huge and shaggy in appearance—at least he seemed so—with a great shock of unruly blond hair and skin so sallow-brown he might have been an Indian. His lips were thick and heavy, and he had dark blue eyes. He looked for all the world as I have always thought the Old Testament prophets must have looked, and when he talked his voice had the low resonant music of a base fiddle. But large in body and magnificent in appearance though he was, evidently his soul had neither largeness or magnificence. That was too bad. Otherwise he might have been a giant among men. But he did want to live, and that was to his favor—except Wes wouldn't let him alone.

"Well now," Wes said, "I have been informed that the sheriff of Brown County has said that Sheriff John Carnes of this county is no sheriff or he would not allow me to stay around Comanche with my murdering pals."

Damn you, Wes, I thought. Just leave it alone and let it be. But Webb was already ahead of me. He had another good answer, maybe one even better than his first one. The problem was he was beginning to play with Wes in the same way Wes was playing with him. I had seen men do that before, and I got uneasy real quick.

"I am not responsible for what the sheriff of Brown County says," Webb replied. "I am only a deputy."

The words came rolling out like deep slow music, but he was just too cocky. I guess a man with all that beauty just never knew how to be any other way. Despite that, it had been a good answer, and I thought, Okay, Wes, this has gone far enough. The man has backed down. Now let him alone so he can walk out with some dignity. I was just about to say something when Dave Carnes beat me to it.

"Men," he said, stepping in between them, "there can be no difference among you about John Carnes."

Carnes put his hand on each man's shoulder, looking from one to the other. Then he turned to Charley Webb.

"Mr. Webb, let me introduce you to Mr. Hardin."

Thank God and may He bless you, Dave Carnes, I thought, but Wes had seen something I hadn't.

"What is that you have in your hand, Mr. Webb?" Wes asked.

It was only then I noticed Webb had his hand behind his back, and suddenly I remembered seeing it there when he first crossed the alley. I unfolded my arms and brought my hand down to rest on the butt of my pistol. By this time a number of men had come into the saloon, including several I did not know. I assumed them to be friends of Webb, and I knew I had to be ready.

Then Webb brought his hand out from behind his back, showing us a half smoked cigar that had gone out. Thank God, I thought again, beginning to relax.

"I am sorry I doubted you, Mr. Webb. We were just going inside to take a drink or have a cigar. Won't you join us?"

"Certainly," Webb said.

Wes then turned back toward the door, meaning to go back inside. Evidently, Webb had been waiting for just this opportunity. As soon as Wes's back was turned, he made his move, but Bud Dixon saw what he intended before he could get his gun out.

"Look out, John!" he cried.

Webb was slowly lifting his pistol out of its holster when Bud hollered, hoping to get it clear before anyone noticed. Looking back, it seemed to me Wes was already turning before Bud hollered. Of course, Webb had his gun out by the time Wes turned and had it pointed on a level with Wes' stomach. To avoid Webb's shot Wes ducked to the left, drawing his pistol and firing as he did so. Webb fired too, maybe at the same time Wes did or perhaps a half second before.

At first, I thought Webb had killed Wes, but the bullet passed through his side just under his ribs and then on out his back. Webb's second shot went wild. Wes's bullet had caught him in the left cheek, below his eye, and he fired as he was falling, as much by reflex as anything else. In the same interval, Jim Taylor and Bud Dixon had pulled their pistols and each fired once at Webb before he hit the ground, not realizing he was already finished.

And so Charley Webb was dead. He had left the county of his jurisdiction and entered another for the unlawful purpose of killing a man he knew only by reputation and who had committed no crime in the county under his charge. He had encountered him, drawn on him when his back was turned and now was dead. No man could blame Wes as no one present had any real question as to who was at fault. At least a dozen witnesses saw what happened, and that should have been the end of it. But, of course, it wasn't.

It was close to an hour before we could get out of town. In the interim Webb's friends and a large group of local citizens managed to burn down my brother's blacksmith shop and to shoot him dead, knowing I was pinned down inside the saloon along with Wes and couldn't do anything about it. Likely, the mob would have gone on to kill the rest of us but for the timely intervention of Wes's father and his old bear dog and for the bravery of Sheriff John Carnes. We were but six and could not have hoped to stand off the fifty or so who were against us, but it was Mr. Hardin who turned the tide. He came roaring into town, scaring hell out of the whole bunch of them, and then the dog exploded into their advance on the saloon, upending them like bottles. That turn of events gave the sheriff what he needed to get the drop on the mob and gave us our chance to get out of town. That Wes failed to mention his father's role or that of the dog in his account of his life and to give an inaccurate view of what followed the shooting of Webb was at first a puzzlement to me. Then I realized he wanted to protect what relatives might still reside in and around Comanche, and he knew an accurate accounting of that day's events would only open old wounds and excite the passions of his enemies. These deliberate inaccuracies and omissions in Wes's account of his life have had another effect as well. They corroborate the misinformation put out by the mob in the days following Webb's death rather than the facts as I remember them, with the result that all publications on the matter I have examined are likewise inaccurate and misleading. I will mention only one example—the mob never disarmed the Reverend Hardin or Sheriff John Carnes or his deputy Frank Wilson as they claimed, and of course they never acknowledged the Reverend Hardin's role in the gun fight on the square or that of his dog.

As soon as we could get to our horses, we rode west to Round Mountain about four miles out to hide until it was safe for us to leave the county. But almost before we entered the cover at the base of the mountains a Ranger captain by the name of Bill Waller and over five hundred men were already beginning to look for us. Despite the fading light, from the top of that large and flat-topped mountains we could see them leave Comanche and start our way. The dust cloud looked a mile wide, and all those horses running sounded like thunder.

"I wished I was back in Comanche right now," Bud Dixon said.

"Why?" Jim Taylor asked him.

"Cause there can't be nobody else there," he said. "They're all riding with old Bill Waller."

It was the way we all felt, including Wes.

We stayed in the vicinity of Round Mountain for close to five days, having numerous encounters with these vigilantes but always managing to escape. Though they could have closed in on us at any time, they had too much respect for Wes to try anything rash, assuming, I suspect, that a dozen or more of them might die if they tried to rush us. Mostly we just sat up there on the mountain and watched them ride in circles around us. Whenever they got too close, we would shoot a couple of

their horses out from under them, and at night we would slip
out through their watch posts for water and food. Of course,
they could not stop us for fear of killing their own people.
Firing wild shots in the dark where five hundred men are
camped didn't make much sense. Finally, Wes decided that
we should separate and leave the county.

Even if Wes had not made the decision to split up, I had
already decided I was through. It had become apparent to me
that Wes would never change and, whether his fault or not,
that he would always be running from one kind of trouble or
another. By that time I received confirmation about my
brother's death, and knowing that I was in part responsible
was a most cruel blow. On top of that it had been an
unnecessary death. Wes could have disarmed Webb as easily
as he shot him, but he didn't. Somehow, he had to prove
something. I don't know what—just one more time, just one
more death. Maybe his father was right. Maybe it was that
name.

"Hell, Mr. Hardin," I told the old man once, "a few
Methodists and Baptists killing each other over in England
don't make a war, not a full scale religious war—"

"Wesleyans and Calvinists!" he thundered. "And a holy,
bloody war it most certainly was, laying waste the whole
islands and a part of the continent too and all because of a
name—that name!"

Maybe he was right.

But you can see my thinking. My five years with Wes had
brought me nothing but trouble, and my reputation was on
the increase simply from association, making it unsafe for me
to walk the streets of a number of towns in Texas. My older
brother had just been savagely murdered, and I still had a
younger brother and sister living in Comanche as well as my
brother's wife and children. I resolved to go back there and
try to make a life for myself, and so I did. Though it was
another five years before the taint of being Wes's friend wore
off enough to allow me to come and go as I pleased, I have
never been sorry. For me the violence and fear eventually came

to an end. For Wes it never stopped.

It ended for others too. The day I came back to Comanche I learned that a mob led by Bill Waller or one of his associates had killed the Hardin's Negro cook, Julie Ola Faye, who had always treated me well. They found her naked a half mile or so from the Hardin home, down near her own house, with blood smeared all over her body from a hog she had killed and was dressing out when they rode up. She had always been a striking woman, and the man who told me about the murder said a half dozen of the mob got it in their heads to rape her but when they got down off their horses to try, first she started singing and then she pulled a couple of Wes's old pistols out of the carcass of the hog and shot twelve times into the middle of armed men and their horses without scoring a single hit. Instead of raping her, they shot her. A short time later the mob hanged Wes's brother Joe along with three of our common friends.

But I never blamed Wes for what happened anymore than I blamed myself. He was always just what he was and I knew that. It had been my decision to stay with him as long as I did, and he never tried to hold me. Besides, I figure he had his share of grief, and when I heard he had been captured in Florida and brought back to Texas for trial and then sentenced to Huntsville, I was relieved for him. I hoped he now would be able to lead a life of relative peace and contentment and that he would be given the recognition he deserved for all he had done for the state of Texas.

But though Wes was a hero to many around the state, he was a man whose time had passed. Texas was changing, and it had no use for a Wes Hardin any longer, hero or not. It had wanted its Sam Houstons and Davy Crocketts and Travises and Bowies in their time, but now it wanted them only in the form of statues and on the pages of history books. By 1874 any one of these great heroes of the Republic, alive and given the same courage and personality and stature he had enjoyed in his prime, would have been an embarrassment to the state just as Wes Hardin was an embarrassment. Still I believed that once Wes had served his time and was released he would finally be able to lead the normal life which had been denied him for so long and maybe go into the practice of law as his brother and father had done.

When I opened the paper in the smoking car of the train and saw that Wes had been killed and read under what circumstances, I knew I had been wrong. Though I felt no grief at Wes's death, I was truly shocked. It was as though I was reading about the death of a stranger, and I found myself caught up in the wonder of it just as the gentlemen around me. A great and famous man had died. Although not a good man as we commonly think of good men, he was a legend and had been for over twenty years.

That day on the train, I almost gave in to my old need to share Wes's life. I wanted to tell those fine cultured gentlemen who I was and just what kind of man Wes had been, but I backed out. It was his life, and it had never really been mine, no matter how hard I tried to pretend otherwise. Had I told them my story it would have been as an interloper in his story just as I had been one in his life. It was best that I keep what I knew to myself and so I did and have done, until now.

It's strange how legends grow, almost out of nothing sometimes, but Wes's was no fluke. He earned every bit of notoriety attributed to him and missed getting a great deal more that he deserved. Even the people of Comanche, who back there in 1874 would have destroyed their whole town to get their hands on him, later came to see him as an asset to the history of the town and county. Had they been able to hang him, I'm sure their anger would have been short lived, maybe not even lasting through the day. They might even have taken his body down and carefully washed and dressed him and then buried him with all due honor. Perhaps they would even have wept at his death the way he always insisted people would do. Later they might have put up a marble monument in his honor, reading HERE LIES JOHN WESLEY HARDIN, FAMOUS HERO OF THE EARLY TEXAS FRONTIER, A MAN LOVED AND RESPECTED BY ALL.

BORN BONHAM, TEXAS, MAY 26th, 1853.   DIED COMANCHE, TEXAS, MAY 26th, 1874.

In particular, I remember an incident that occurred some years after I had settled in Comanche to make my home. A small boy of about ten who lived in the house next to mine had spent his youth to then playing cowboys and Indians and outlaws. While he would consent to being an Indian and getting shot and killed and occasionally to taking the part of Billy the Kid or Sam Bass, he would under no circumstances play John Wesley Hardin or participate in any reenactment of Hardin's Comanche County shootout. He had been half raised to that time by his grandfather who had attempted to insure his model behavior by threatening to send John Wesley Hardin and his nasty gang of cutthroats after him if he didn't mind what he was told. Over and over he was reminded of Hardin's diabolical exploits in the town of Comanche and of the just end he had come to as a resident of the state penitentiary in Huntsville. Perhaps because of these early teachings the boy was close to his mother and protective of her. On the day that she surrendered her life in church and declared she was saved, her son got it in his head that the preacher in his black coat was John Wesley Hardin and that the Reverend intended to do his mother harm. He had learned just enough church lore to connect the John Wesley of religion with the John Wesley Hardin of recent Texas history, and he watched over his mother all the rest of that day and the week that followed, not allowing her friends from the church to come anywhere near her. Despite her repeated explanations, he refused to believe she was not in danger and not the victim of some dark conspiracy only he by his resourcefulness and quick thinking had been able to discover and hence to frustrate.

Finally, he consented to allowing her to be baptized in a near-by creek after repeated assurances from her that baptism would not harm her and was indeed what she truly desired. But when he saw the preacher take her by the head and push her under the water, he knew he had been tricked and his old fears returned. All those years of being told John Wesley

Hardin would get him if he didn't behave himself coalesced into a single horrifying image. Believing himself once more to be his mother's only chance and the preacher and his followers to be escaped killer John Wesley Hardin and his gang, he picked up a long stick and jumped off the creek bank into the water, catching the preacher in the mouth and knocking out four of his teeth. When afterwards they had to restrain him to keep him from drowning the stunned preacher, he looked up at them with half-crazed, tear-reddened eyes and cried out, "Now shoot me, you horse racing sons of bitches! Now hang me, you poker-playing bastards you!"

4/97   2 3/97
2/04   4   7/98